Bring the Dawn

short stories and poems of hope and joy

Dixie Ann Black

www.Dixieannblack.com

Dixie Ann Black
Enterprises

Tallahassee, FL

Dixie Ann Black Enterprises
Tallahassee, FL
(850) 556-6983

Visit our website at: www.DixieAnnBlack.com

Email us at: DixieAnnBlack@gmail.com

Cover Design by: aJuxt Media Group

ISBN: 978-0-692-69063-5

LCCN: 2016906559

First printing, April 2016, USA

Table of Contents

5

Valentine Vendetta

When the cops arrived Claire was sprawled on the floor of the supermarket's candy aisle with a mountain of empty chocolate wrappers around her.

A bomb had exploded in her life. Phil had left her two days before Valentine's Day. The cheap bastard! Nine years; nine years and 363 days of her life she had given him and in all that time he had never even bought her a decent Valentine's Day present. Now here was the final insult; with only two days to go before their 10th anniversary he had dumped her. He had mumbled some lame excuse about needing to find himself, but she knew the truth.

She had walked around in a daze for two days feeling disconnected from her routine. She hadn't been to work, she hadn't showered, she hadn't eaten. Hunger finally penetrated her stupor and led her to the supermarket. That's when it hit her that this was in fact Valentine's Day, the day of her aborted 10th anniversary. All around her men were buying last minute flowers, balloons and chocolates. Everybody was happy but her. She didn't remember tearing all the candy off the shelves and would have denied eating several pounds of assorted chocolates if it wasn't for the smearings of M & M's, Godiva, Lindt and several others all over her face and hands.

The police had been summoned after she had refused to leave the aisle, pelting the store employees with gum balls and other hard candies each time they approached her. The manager had dared to ignore the flying missiles and actually grabbed her by one arm but he had been forced to retreat when she sank her chocolate coated incisors into his hand. He was a mild mannered man. The bite coupled with a significant injury to his eye from a lollipop had delivered his defeat.

In an attempt at discretion, shoppers had been ushered to the cash registers at the far end of the store; because, Lord forbid, the store would actually close its doors on Valentine's Day due to a psychotic woman on a rampage and miss the opportunity for increased revenue. The two officers had approached from opposite ends of the aisle, their hands hovering over their holsters. But when they saw the disheveled brown haired woman sitting on the floor, her red skirt askew with candy wrappers rapidly mounting over her extended legs they both relaxed their stances and stared. She seemed oblivious of their company as she shoved Reese's peanut butter cups and Cadbury eggs into her mouth. Pity and amusement vied for expression on their countenances as they approached her. Claire had returned to her senses enough to realize she should not pelt the officers but she remained seated, refusing their command to get up like a recalcitrant two year old in the middle of a tantrum.

The kinder of the two officers, thinking he was taking a gentler approach said, "Lady, it's Valentine's Day. Wouldn't you rather be eating your candy at home with your sweetheart?" At the utterance of the lethal combination: "Valentine's Day" and "Sweetheart", Claire burst into a fit of bawling, the likes of which the officers had never before witnessed. No amount of pleading or threats could overcome her tears. The curious shoppers were becoming unnerved as the wailing echoed through the store like the dying of a prehistoric beast. The officers, not quite sure how to handle a situation that called for professional psychological intervention, shifted uncomfortably from one foot to the other waiting and hoping that the spell would pass.

That's when Phil happened to enter the store. It was one of those coincidences that made one believe in fate for he was unaware that Claire was in the store and had no inkling of her mental and emotional state. He therefore had no idea he was taking his life in his hands when he ignored the store manager's discrete encouragement to avoid the candy aisle. A stingy man, with thoughts only of personal gain, Phil was intent on grabbing the

limp petals of the left over flowers along with a box of chocolates
for under $20. He felt sure this would secure the affections of his
new love. He was wrong of course, but he had skated along by
cheap and selfish means for over nine years so he could not foresee
that his lack of deep sentiment would be his undoing.

Being a generally unconscious man he paid no heed to the eerie
howl. Surely he heard it but since he figured it did not affect him it
certainly did not concern him. He strode determinedly into the
candy aisle like an idiot into the cage of a hungry lion. For one
precious moment Claire's tears clouded her vision suspending the
sentence of her defiler. But in the moment it took for that precious
droplet to fall through her lashes and unto the supermarket floor,
the life of her recently removed lover was changed and rearranged.

The officers had one story and the nosey patrons another, Phil
would claim them both untrue but the manager had the best view.
He later reported that the woman descended on the unsuspecting
man like a hail storm in summer. She swooped down upon his
meager frame twisting him like a leaf in the centrifugal force of a
tornado. Then she sat on his sad and twisted body and pummeled
him with the ferocity of an insane beast. Once the vengeful lust of
the tigress began to abate the officers recovered themselves enough
to move from their petrified state. Concerned that they may have
somehow dishonored the badge they wore, they yelled words like
"Halt!" and "Back away from the body Ma'am!" in deep manly
voices. But it was too late for poor Phil. He was not dead. Oh no,
but at that moment he wished with all his heart to be in that final
rest. He had peed his pants in fear when she had pounced on him
like a tigress trapping a mouse. And since it was his nature to flee,
being caught left him without the option of bravery.

Claire did step away from his bruised and battered frame but not
before she whispered a threat in his ear. It must have been a
powerful threat indeed because poor Phil immediately clutched his
groin and limped to his feet with the help of an abandoned grocery

cart calling out to the officers as they circled Claire. In a desperate and high pitched tone he pleaded that they let her go. The fault was his and his alone. He would pay for the mess they had made and no blame should rest on Claire. He explained to the officers with earnest that although they did not see, he had issued the first blow and poor Claire had only defended herself. The fact that she stood to the side disheveled but totally unscathed licking her lips like a cat after devouring a mouse did not dissuade Phil from spinning his tale. In fact her confidence seemed to spur a frenzy in him to be believed. Yes, he said. He had been abusing her for years so please lock him up instead, he pleaded.

The officers stared at him in consternation then at each other. They glanced over at Claire and with a shudder, quickly glanced away. It was the manager who finally saved the moment. He was anxious to regain control of his store and saw an opportunity to please his superiors.

"You said you are willing to pay for the damage?" he asked Phil. When Phil quickly bobbed his head like a wind-up toy and reached for his wallet the manager seized the moment.

"Officers, there is no longer a problem here. All parties are agreed." The manager announced with new found authority in his voice. The officers looked at each other and shrugged. Less paperwork, they figured. Then they sauntered toward the exit but they were careful to stay on the opposite side of the aisle from poor abused Claire. One of them mumbled something about a Tasmanian devil but only Phil heard his words. The store manager flooded with energy from his new found relief, dashed off to get the appropriate paperwork.

And just like that Phil found himself face to face with Claire, with nothing behind him but empty candy wrappers. The space between them however, was charged with the energy of a battlefield. (Although in fact it had been more like a single handed act of carnage.) He peered at her through his quickly swelling eye lids, ignoring the stings that came from where she had pierced his flesh

9

with her acrylic nails. His heart pounded in his ears, his mind screamed run! but his legs refused to go.

Claire had been staring at him, brows creased in a deep frown; lips puckered in an angry pout. She stood with her head held high, most of her ample weight distributed on her back leg, her arms folded. When she shifted and let her arms fall to her side Phil flinched and beads of moisture formed at the corners of his eyes. A soft disjointed melody filled the space between them. When the sound penetrated his fears he realized she was speaking to him through her own tears.

"You were right you know," she was saying, "You have abused me all these years.
"Sure, you never hit me but you were always so selfish and unkind. But still I loved you with all of me; despite your unkind ways. You were my hero Phil." She paused as if to let the immensity of that role sink in. Then she added, "And you destroyed that love Phil. I know about that girl. You didn't have the guts to tell me the truth. Do you think she will love a coward? What about a cheapskate who won't shell out the money for a decent gift?
"Your scars will heal Phil. But I hope they leave a mark so that each time you see them you can see the scars you left on my heart." She walked up to him and he steeled himself for another attack. But she gently tugged on the abandoned grocery cart he had been clinging to, giving him time to regain his balance as she pulled it away. In it were the groceries she had selected before she had entered the candy aisle. She calmly completed her shopping, used the self-checkout lane and walked out the door.

When Phil walked into work the next morning he was a few minutes late because he had gone to great pains to hide the evidence of his violent encounter the night before. He needn't have bothered. He tried to slip in unnoticed but he worked in a large open area of a state accounting office so he was hard to miss. His coworkers were huddled in small groups around their cell phones. Someone in the supermarket the night before had taken a video of the beat down and posted it on YouTube. It had gone viral with the caption "Valentine Vendetta".

John was the first to approach him with a venomous glee. "Man, looks like a sistah put a hurting on you last night." There was no love lost between them, so John was quick to claim the upper hand. Phil was the "go to" numbers geek in the office but John preferred to get by on his ability to use others. In keeping with his frugality Phil was not about to let anyone use him. He had taken it to the next level, pointing out John's shortcomings to management thus earning John's unrelenting hatred. "There's no way I'd let a woman beat me down like that." John had said the last sentence loud enough for the entire office to hear. Phil swallowed hard, straightened his aching back and swiveled his chair around to the suddenly urgent numbers on his computer screen. All day long the men in the office offered jabs. The women snickered or smirked as they walked by. Unlike the men, they didn't ask why or how this had happened. They knew exactly why. He was known among the ladies as a stingy and anal man and now his sins had come home to roost.

Any hope Phil had of keeping his humiliation from his new flame was thwarted by the World Wide Web. His Facebook page, which he had heretofore kept as a testament to his self-avowed masculine prowess, was a hot zone of fiery comments. Someone had shared the YouTube video directly unto his page. Someone else had commented. It was downhill from there. The video had over 300 "likes" before the day was out and one of them was Sheila, his now aborted love interest. It did not help that he had not showed up or called the night before. Once he left the supermarket he had rushed home to minimize his humiliation. Any thought of salvaging the evening had disappeared once he looked in the mirror. He faced looked as if he had been stung by an army of killer bees. He had thought of calling Sheila with an excuse but he couldn't come up with anything that sounded plausible to his own ears.

In the end he had stripped himself of his shame, dropped the evidence into the washing machine and taken a hot shower. He had downed a couple of shots of cheap vodka before crawling into bed. He had lain there all night, the scenes of his life playing before him like an accusing documentary. At heart he was a logical man. An eye was always balanced by an eye, a tooth by another tooth. Try as he might he could not blame Claire. His mistake had been his assumption that she was weaker than him. He had been convinced that the bravado he sported had covered his insecurities but now all he could see was Claire's tear stained face asking him "Do you think she will love a coward?"
Yes, he was to blame but he could see no way out of his shame. When sleep came it was froth with nightmarish anxieties. He was naked and running for his life, shame and humiliation like land mines as he hurtled along in the darkness of his dreams.

The next morning he awoke like a man on the day of his execution. He instinctively knew he had come to the end of himself. He had two choices: treat "the incident" as if it never happened and let his bravado carry him along, remaining unconscious to any lessons it might have offered; or he could die. Die to the fears that had so long held him and see what life was like beyond his fears. True to his cowardice he decided to flaunt his bravado like a new suit. Surely this would blow over soon. He grabbed the Fedora he believed made him look suave, covering his puffy eyes with the rim of the hat then he headed for the door of his miserable apartment. His intent was to deny his own culpability long enough for the excitement to fade. His choice was made. He needn't have bothered for as it turned out life had already made the choice for him.

It happened that Phil was good at one thing; accounting. In fact he was a wiz with numbers. The truth be known, he preferred numbers to people. A five was always a five, it never pretended to be a six or faked being a ten. He knew where he stood with numbers. But his coworkers typically agonized over the math portions of their job. John in particular struggled in getting two fives to equal 10. He got by based on his good looks and bold assertions. Just before each yearly audit he would sweet talk one of the newer women in the office to help him straighten out his incomplete and inaccurate balance sheets. The rigid math requirements of the job ensured that there was never a shortage of new faces in the office thus supplying him with an ever refreshing pool of potential saps. Most new employees would initially underestimate their mathematical prowess, gladly taking on extra duties to prove themselves; then experience a rude awakening by the time of their first review. By the six month mark they would be sheepishly cleaning out their desks for the final time. Phil had watched them come and go over the last 10 years with childlike fascination. As with many gifted people he could not understand why they found something as straightforward as math to be difficult. And, as with many gifted people, he was woefully socially imbalanced and therefore unable to use his gift to his advantage with people. He was an abysmal failure with the ladies. He would have remained a solitary nerd if Claire had not pursued him. Recently Sheila had shone the light of her affections on him and he had lost all sense of reason, quickly abandoning Claire emotionally for the attentions of the new office beauty. He convinced himself that he had found someone who was attracted to him for his brilliance and dedication. In a sense he was correct as he was, in a very narrow sense, a brilliant and dedicated man.

Not so with John Walford. He was no wiz, but a very average man, and as such had full access to the wiles that brought him his desires. In the seven years he had worked in that position he had perfected his ability to leech off his coworkers and so remain in good standing with his supervisors. When new employees were rare John would lean on his older peers to help him with his work. This is how Phil had been able to bring his ineptitude to management's attention. To the dismay of Phil and his coworkers

John's supervisor was a bottom-line kind of guy who only cared about outcomes. The fact that John's slothfulness resulted in hours of revisions for those who relied on his data each year did not concern him as long as he got the outcome he wanted; a successful yearly audit. But there were several new recruits this year so John defaulted to his proven plan to excel in the yearly audit. It didn't matter much that some of the new female employees were often challenged by complex math and unsure of themselves. In fact this was to his advantage. His plan simply required them to enter data into the system and let the Excel spreadsheets prompt them when they were unsure. This was a time consuming and sometimes complex feat that had some employees working late nights to stay caught up. But while his coworkers agonized over balancing each cent and getting reports completed on time John relied on last minute catching up. In this way he survived the annual audits. His desire to avoid the challenge of his job led him to risk incorrect data entry and skewed reports.

The new employee John generally focused on was usually lacking confidence and was not typically the smartest of the new recruits. She was however always pretty. Deceived by the assumption that her looks bestowed special honor she was led enthusiastically and without question to the slaughter by flattery and promise. She would be "learning the system", "getting brownie points" and "getting special privileges" from her firmly ensconced benefactor. Two months before the annual audit each September John would curtail his office romance and set to work reviewing and recalculating the data his unwitting helper had entered. He would spit out monthly reports that had been neglected, correct entries that his subjects had unknowingly entered in the wrong categories and generally cook the books to let it appear that he had done all the work in a timely and accurate manner. To his lazy mind two months of hard work was better than nine months of painstaking data entry and calculations. This would of course have the effect of making all reports previously ran from his original data entry incorrect. His love interest would then find herself responsible for

14

updating and correcting her own work and explaining any errors to her supervisor. By the time the ruse was uncovered she would be busy struggling to keep her own job and scarcely had time to address being used. Unfortunately, the woman John chose for this year's dubious honor of pack mule was among the prettiest and brightest. She was none other than the recently stood up Sheila Boone.

When Phil entered the office John had already began to make his move. Sheila was a curvaceous brown skinned girl who was pretty enough for all the men to notice her and smart enough to secure a permanent position without favors, so her reasons for yielding to John's tired scheme escaped Phil. With reasoning typical of ego-based insight he assumed she was using John to get back at him for their botched romance. John didn't think that deeply. Snatching Phil's love interest and using her for his yearly audit catch up would be a double boon. So John threw himself into the role of seducer. He splayed himself across the corner of Sheila's desk attempting to impress her with his best material; his recount of his glory days as a high school running back on the then undefeated team. Twenty years had passed and the team had been renamed after a five year losing streak but John was still living in that moment when his fancy footwork, speed and skill delivered the state championship. Unfortunately, the former football star had not taken the time to properly vet his intended conquest. If he had, he would have known that Sheila had some records of her own. Unlike her male counterpart she maintained her physique through routine workouts and her lifestyle through easy marks like John. She had set her sights on Phil until the "beat-down" debacle. She had decided Phil was either too dumb or too much in the public's eye for her immediate plans. So when Mr. Almost Heisman had decided to shower her with his attention she had made a snap decision to take it; All of it.

In the weeks that followed Sheila and John became a hot new item. She would stay after hours entering his data. John stayed too, for the first hour or so. He would inevitably dust off one of his well-rehearsed excuses as to why he had to go, then leave her in the office alone, having given her the security code reserved for permanent staff so she could lock up. But he would show up the next morning with a single fresh cut red rose duly moistened or an exquisitely wrapped box of chocolates, or a stuffed animal holding forth its joyous red heart for her to hold. Sheila would be at the office when he arrived, showing no signs of strain from her late nights. She would receive the Coach handbags, the Jimmy Chu stilettos and all the gifts she requested with soft brown smiles and at lunch time the two would disappear for the hour.

The annual audit was the gauntlet that determined the fates of the new recruits as well as the established employees for whom numbers were a chore. It was also the standard by which raises were determined or exit plans were made. Unfortunately for John Walford, the annual auditors arrived one morning in July, unannounced and unexpectedly early; almost two months early. John was beside himself with worry. He had not had a chance to reconcile the data. He tried to look unconcerned but he worked alone every evening until well into the night trying to get information reconciled before the auditors pulled his reports.

The audit always lasted five days with an exit on the fifth day. This was that day. It had been a grueling week of stone faced auditors asking for documentations, calculations, and justifications. Excel spreadsheets were printed in sheaves while the company's computerized accounting system froze intermittently from the strain of the increased demands. The entire staff, including Sheila had been at the beck and call of the auditors. Phil had been in hyper-nerd mode, producing the information requested with relish. Today he arrived in mud brown slacks and a rumpled white shirt which looked suspiciously like an unwashed version of the one he wore two days before. All week John had frowned repeatedly when back up documentation had been requested of him. But today he was resplendent in his confidence. He was wearing his charcoal grey suit with the sage green shirt and blood red tie, the outfit he reserved for the last day of the annual audit. Sheila walked in wearing an apple red dress which clung tightly to her curves and threatened the boundaries of professional attire. Phil's mouth went dry at the sight of her but John, who was busy trying to maintain a facade of calm, seemed not to notice. He alternated between brushing imaginary lint off his suit and striking thoughtful poses as they waited for the exit interview with the auditors.

The audit summary was conducted in a drab little box known as the conference room. Had it been a few square feet smaller it could have been mistaken for a solitary confinement cubicle. There were no windows and no paintings adorned the drab institutional paint. The grayish white color brought to mind a wasteland from which no one escaped. The most offensive feature was the lack of an air conditioning return vent, making the box as airless as a tomb.

The team of six auditors dispensed with the preliminary findings and mercifully let half of the accounting team leave the stuffy little room with their notes on the minor correction to follow. This left another twelve people to sweat it out in an airless 10x12 room while their specific areas were reviewed in detail. Phil who was well versed on these proceedings noticed that something appeared to be amiss. He was always in the room throughout the entire summary and knew the order in which each person or department head was reviewed and excused. The new hires assigned to the accounting department had been dismissed after the general findings were announced. They would be reviewing the details of their individual fates with their particular supervisors. But Sheila, also a new hire, was still in the room. She sat exuding an air of confidence that bordered on arrogance. John meanwhile was developing sweat rings under the armpits of his suit as his turn approached.

The auditors began this section by calling the individual accounting specialist's name before reviewing the findings. "John Walford."

John bolted to attention in his seat, sweat beats forming on his brow. An auditor opened a file three inches thick with papers. He waded through them silently. The air grew even thicker. The beads of sweat on John's brow began to fall unto his grey suite. After what seemed to John like the sun's entire journey around the earth he heard the auditor say, "Mr. Walford can you explain to us the many discrepancies in your data?" He held out the hefty record of John's wrongs obviously waiting for him to take it. John stood up, his knees weak. He walked slowly to the front of the room and took the file from the auditor. The weight seemed to surprise him and he lost his grip. The file slid to the floor sending scores of papers floating in all directions.

Sheila had been sitting seemingly creating her own cool while everyone else became clammy. "Maybe I can be of some help here." She uncrossed her legs, stood up and approached the front of the room. John's face was panic stricken. He didn't know whether to bend down and try to pick up the papers or violently wave his hands to tell Sheila to say nothing. Having wrong calculations was one thing, having a new employee confess to entering your classified data was an entirely different level of wrong doing.

He managed a squeak "That's all right Ms. Boone."

"Actually, it's not!" Sheila's voice was smooth as melted chocolate as she took center stage.

"It has come to the attention of the Federal Trade Commission that this office has been engaging in questionable accounting for some time now."

John looked confused. Phil tried to follow. He noticed that the supervisors in the room showed no surprise. Sheila continued,

"I have been a part of an undercover operation to find out why there has been a pattern of extensive revisions in the accounting department of this office each year around this time." Suddenly the numbers all added up in Phil's mind. John was a little slower on the uptake.

"Whaat?" he was genuinely confused as he had never considered that his actions may affect anyone beyond his whiny co-workers. "What are you talking about and what does it have to do with me?"

John's plaintive cry was almost pitiable. Phil shook his head in disbelief.

It took a painstakingly long time for John to understand that he had been the subject of a sting operation; that Sheila was in fact an undercover agent and that he was in fact in bigger trouble than just being late on this year's balance sheets. Apparently one or more of those women he had used along the way had blown the whistle. When the FTC came calling his supervisors had not hesitated in throwing him to the wolves. Sheila in the meantime had made the best of her role. She had been wined and dined and showered with presents, and in the end she had still gotten her man. As the agents escorted John out of the building Sheila slipped the strap of her Coach purse over her shoulder and strutted out of the building on her Jimmy Chu stilettos.

Phil felt a chill run through him as he watched her leave. He knew his work was good but a woman like that delighted in capturing her prey. She would have found a way to make him pay. He shuddered again, this time visibly. Then a thought, warm as the morning sun entered his heart. He flipped open his cell phone, dialed and put it up to his ear.

"Claire, I know. I know. I was so wrong. But I'd like to make it up to you Claire. Can we start over? Can I take you shopping, my treat?"

Everywhere

*I couldn't see you till you left
Now you're not here.
But you are all I see everywhere.*

I Love Love

I love love but I don't love the tears
Drenching the negligee I wore for you to see
Wondering what will become of me.
Isn't love supposed to ease the fears?
Shouldn't it last throughout the years?

I love love but I don't love its painful hold
There's no tenderness in control
What happens to us when I say no?
Who will hold me when you go?

I love love but its captivity suffocates me.
Is there a love that sets me free?
Or is it illusion sold as truth?
Opiate for the lonely, game for the youth?

I love love but I will walk alone
Silence filling the empty spaces I made for you
Freed from the mirage of a 'you and me'
Opening to a greater revelation of me.

Nefarious Love

Shirtless and dripping he came to her like a god,
fresh from the raging seas.
Wild with passion, wanton with wanting,
consuming every part of her;
Taking her body to rape her soul,
he was the devil, but beautiful to behold.

Bring the Dawn

When his passions were abated,
his beauty would turn to stone.
He held no joy beyond his lust,
no interest beyond his carnal fires
And when she spoke of Heavenly things,
he'd seduce her with desires.

This god-man covered her quivering flesh
with the beauty of his own
He reach inside her sacred space to tear the alter down
He sought her heart, her body, mind, to claim them as his crown.

He loves her, hurts her, hates her, bleeds her,
Then he cries and says he needs her
But his love can never free her, it goes no farther than his desire.
His beautiful body vile as sin is his unholy throne.
A wanton delight that seeks the light it can never own.
The depravity of love is no love at all
but fallen faith and empty sound.

What Kind of Love?

There's healing in love,
Not that addicting kind of love.
There is a safe place in love,
Not that lusting kind of love.
There's patience in love,
Not that 'I've got to have you now' kind of love.
So slow your roll and find this space, if this is love.

There's peace in love,
Not that 'all night arguing' kind of love.
There's promise in love,
Not that 'fear of losing you' kind of love.
There's hope in love

Bring the Dawn

Not that 'Oh my God he's found somebody new!' kind of love.
So hold up, let's find out if this is the true kind of love.

There's faith in love,
Not that 'You better not be cheating on me' kind of love.
There a refuge in love,
Not that 'I can't tell you my secrets' kind of love.
There's goodness in love,.
Not that 'He's no good for me but I need him' kind of love.
So let's take a minute and see what's in it,
in this thing we're calling love.

Dreaming

I walk in and there you are, the sun of my constellation.
Our eyes meet and I am falling, seeking my destination
The sparks are flying, my fears are dying, I am falling into you.
I felt your touch pulling me in to you as our eyes met
I orbit you, my lodestar,
I fall through your eyes into the endless depths of me
Finding my beginning in your unending smile.
Your love walks in and rescues me for this sacrificial fire
I long for you, I live for you in the mystery of desire
Your loving passion seals my heart and bonds us in this mystery
And when the fire has burned away the dross of time,
I'll sing to you and hold you close in the joy of this reunion
Of finding myself in you.

Personal Freedom

There is often times a desolation in freedom
not unlike the wide open space of a desert with no relief in sight
But I'd rather be alone in that desert
than imprisoned by someone else's philosophy.
There is also a selfishness in freedom
not tied to the demands of pleasing another's ego
while your own needs go untended.
But I must cultivate my own soul to offer strength to another.
And most of all there is a growth in freedom,
not the tentative superficial type of growing;
But a gut wrenching soul transformation
that can only be birthed in the darkness of being alone.

Don't Say It

Let us not say that word anymore,
You know the one.
It speaks of the mystery of our oneness
And tells us of our deep belonging.
But we use it to separate, based on our preferences
We imbue it with carnality to define our lusts.
We use it to say who is accepted in our eyes
And who is on the other side.
Let us not say that word anymore
But live it, be it
In action and in thought
Let us never say Love again
But exude it from our very being.

Belly Up

Belly up to the Bar of Being
Taking deep draughts of the ale of Now
Savouring each sip
Sharing each breath
With age old Friends;
Silence and Contemplation.

Beauty Treatment

There are few lures more tempting to a middle aged woman than a beauty treatment that promises youthful results. Having crested the hill of youth I found the benefits offered by Japan's many hot springs to be both exciting and seductive. During my recent visit to Japan, I was very enthusiastic about visiting the hot springs until I explained to my hostess that I had forgotten my bathing suit. My Japanese is limited to "Hello", "Goodbye" and "Thanks" and her English was somewhat limited so it took several attempts for us to understand each other. "No clothes." she had finally explained. "What?" The thought of being completely naked in front of a bunch of strangers did not appeal to me. But in the end my hostess who was nearing 70 made it clear that this was a natural and even revered custom of their culture and their family. The implication here was that it would be an affront if I refused to go. I consider myself pretty open minded so I figured I would give it a try. After all if my 70 year old hosts didn't mind going naked why should I? I was somewhat comforted by the fact that this hot spring was divided into male and female sections. At almost 70 my hostess sported a clear, wrinkle free complexion which she attributed to the hot springs, so I decided to try it.

During my first visit to one such hot spring my expectation of a glowing wrinkle free face was piqued by the ageless beauty of the many Japanese women who sat, comfortable in their own skins exuding unselfconscious radiance. Here is an account of my attempt at discovering ageless beauty:

I walk into a large room which feels like a cross between a locker room and a ladies dressing room. I am immediately confronted by naked bodies of varying sizes and shapes. They walk by, totally unconcerned by my stunned silence. I undress in a corner. I figure being naked and black in a room filled with all Japanese women would be like being a flashing neon sign in a starless night. I stand in the corner alternating between holding my little over sized washcloth at my chest and then lower. I struggle with my tiny shield, seeing no way to preserve my dignity until I realize no one cares. They are all busy dressing or undressing without even a glance in my direction. I am urged out of the corner with the gentle guidance of my daughter's mother in law, who has been the consummate hostess. She is completely undressed and at ease. In halting English she explains the rituals as we proceed. I feel emboldened as we enter the area filled with steaming pools of water from the hot springs.

I shed my wash cloth and my own self-consciousness and prepare to wade into the hot pool with my graceful guide. She is quiet, circumspect and proper, a lady in every way. This is a land of tradition and protocols so I endeavor to imitate her soft steps and quiet voice. On our way to one of the pools she points out a large bowl filled with a white paste-like mixture. It is located next to a barrel filled with hot spring water. There is a large bucket-like ladle on the side of the barrel and my hostess explains that I am to dip the ladle into the crystal clear water and rinse myself before entering the wading pools. I comply. As I rinse myself she explains that the paste is a salt mixture used to rejuvenate the skin. She suggests we apply it to our faces and bodies after we have soaked ourselves in the hot spring. In my mind I can already see my face, wrinkle free and 20 years younger, so I agree enthusiastically. We sit in the hot pools surrounded by nature and I begin to understand that beauty is closely intertwined with relaxation.

After a luxurious soak and heart to heart conversations with total strangers who speak very little English, it is time to apply the salt treatment before we take our final wash.
I scoop up handfuls of the mixture and begin to apply it to the front of my body, being careful to avoid the unmentionable areas while scrubbing with the salt for the youthful appearance I envision. My hostess volunteers to rub the mixture on my back while I work on the rest of my body. I scrub myself vigorously massaging the salt mixture onto my face and chest. I massage salt unto my belly and

arms while she gently but thoroughly rubs my back and shoulders. Then I move lower bending over to do my thighs and legs. Finally I scrub each foot and straighten up to wait the 3-5 minutes she suggests before rinsing off the mixture.

I become aware of a small but rapidly growing problem. The water from my hair is running down my face and there is a slight stinging sensation in my left eye. At this moment I remember another property of salt. Burning. Meanwhile my hostess is still busy giving me a genuinely thorough back massage. It would be rude to stop her abruptly, but the stinging is now a burning. I desperately look for water within reach but by now my right eye has also begun to burn. I try to wipe my forehead hoping to relieve the increased burning I know will come from the water dripping from my hair, but it is no use. I am beginning to panic. I can no longer see so I flail my arms in front of me hoping to find the large barrel of spring water nearby. God is merciful and my fingers touch the edge. My hostess is still massaging my back, oblivious of my dilemma. By now both eyes are burning. And my desperate hands cannot find the scoop. There is an order and a method to everything here. I am sure I cannot plunge my salty hands into the pristinely pure barrel of spring water but I have to do something - FAST. Now both eyes are on fire but my oblivious hostess is still spreading salt over neck and shoulders.

My eyes are now roaring volcanos of burning pain. I can't see to run screaming and I don't have the words in Japanese to explain my dilemma. So I plunge my salty hands into the hot water bringing quick handfuls to my eyes. It is not helping. The salt has soaked in and I am sure I will go blind or die from the burning. My hostess is finishing up her generous massage and turning to complete her own salt massage. She has no idea I am in Hell. I splash more water, no longer caring who sees me contaminate their previously pure barrel. My inferno of burning salt has become my only concern.
Finally, relief grudgingly arrives as I furiously and repeatedly

splash my face, and I begin to regain my sight enough to walk with some dignity to the bathing station. Over my shoulder I hear my hostess' gentle voice advising me, "Wait about 3 to 5 minutes!" She doesn't understand that it has already been a lifetime. I slump my naked salted body unto the tiny stool and reach for the faucet, spraying myself directly in the face to completely remove my beauty treatment.

Sighing, I resign myself to live with the wrinkles.
At least for now.

Definitions

Sweet, soft, silky petals falling
The flower is limp; the seed fallen
Time to redefine true beauty.

Bring the Dawn

The Break-up

My Dear Sweet Chocolate
I don't know how to do this
I don't know what to say
But I must leave you Sweet love
I must be on my way.

Long are the nights I held you in my arms
Savoring your sweetness at the break of dawn
You have been my lover when all have been untrue
You've brought me comfort when I didn't know what to do.
Now I must say goodbye, I won't be seeing you.

Our secret meetings, our desperate love
Have been discovered, we've been found out
Now my jeans don't fit, I'm busting out
So I must leave you though there's none so true
I will miss you, my world will be blue.

It's not just you my sweet dark joy
but your companions those sweet fattening carbs.
They say watch the company you keep
And I've been hanging with you guys quite a heap
Now I look in the mirror and it makes me weep.

So goodbye my delicious friend
Though I hate it, this is the end.

The Heart of the Earth

A droplet of water is complete in and of itself.
It doesn't need another droplet to be water
But it does need another droplet to be a lake
An eagle doesn't need another eagle to be a bird of prey

29

Bring the Dawn

But it does need another eagle to carry on its legacy
A speck of dirt doesn't need another speck to be dirt
But it does need more dirt to form land.
In the same way each of us is complete in and of our own
But we need each other to cause a mighty and lasting movement
in the heart of the earth.

Bitter Strength

Weakness is an insidious thing
It sneaks up on us gently in comfort, complacency and ease.
But strength, that illusive force, is forged in struggle,
In the bitter taste of discipline and in lack.

How Beautiful You Are

When I take off the cloak of sickness and fear
I stand naked in the boldness of a healing love.
Unplugging the earphones of the world's clamor
I listen to the deep stillness of my soul.
It is then that I see how beautiful You are
It is then that I know we are one.

Shifting Ground

Walking on the shifting ground of life's realities,
I plant a foot in Spirit
Moving, swaying, finding balance
It's the dance called life.

The Lamp

Shying away from the stadium lights
Those spotlights that blind
We find the darkness of the uncharted path
We shine the lamp of Truth in our own darkness
And bring forth the creativity of our souls.

Giving Away Diamonds

Searching for diamonds in the coal mines of life
I rejoice when I find a sliver, a shard of beauty.
That's when You tell me that True Beauty
lies in giving away even that sliver.

A Reason To Be

Life's about redemption
or it's a useless lie.
It's about healing
Not just pie in the sky.
Life's about hope
not just what we see
or there'd be no point to you
no reason for me to be.

If a star can live again in dust and wind and trees
why can't I see again though my vision's dim?
there a place for me to be
just beyond this mortal door
a vision of life I've longed for
But never known before.

Bring the Dawn

Matter and energy can never be destroyed
So why should living again be so hard?
there's a place beyond this place
for man to be set free
for the soul to live again
a place to truly be.
There is joy and love and truth after all this pain.
There's sunshine in the opening after every rain.

The Fog

I came upon it suddenly like an accident round the bend.
It blinded me with its persistence
Hiding from view all I knew was there
until I thought to despair.
No clear path to trod, no sunshine,
no familiar markers of progress on my way.
Until the silhouette of an anhinga flying above lifted my eyes and
my spirits
Clearing my inner vision so I could sense the beauty in not being
able to see.

<u>Death View</u>

I died on a Thursday. Damn.

How typical of me to miss the weekend.

I didn't realize it at first. I kept trying to get back home, trying to reach my office, trying to get out of the car stuck on the side of the road. The Jerk who had side-swiped me, had sped by and I couldn't wait to catch up with him and let him know what I thought. I kept fighting with the door of my new blue Mercedes coupe. I couldn't understand why the door wouldn't open. I'd hit that tree and blacked out for a moment but when I came to everything seemed the same. The longer I sat there fiddling with the lock and trying to use my cell phone the more frustrated I got. Nothing worked. The clock on the dashboard had stopped at the time of impact. I figured it shorted out. My cellphone was on roaming, I couldn't get a signal. The door would not unlatch so I figured it was because of the impact. I was trapped inside my car.

When the futility of my efforts registered, frustration turned to panic. I banged on the door and yelled, ignoring the fact that I was on the side of a long, lonely winding highway with only an occasional car whizzing by. I gradually started to notice little things, like the way I would grip the steering wheel but not really feel it, and the way I beat on the window but not feel the soreness that should have set in from the sustained pounding. Then there was the daylight. It was early evening when the Jerk ran me off the road. I had spent hours trying to get out, even in my panic I knew a lot of time must have passed but the fading sunlight never changed. Night did not come.

As realization dawned my heart started racing, I started to sweat, I was losing my mind, I was sure. Then I realized I thought I was sweating but my brow was dry except for the sticky place on my temple that had oozed blood when I hit the tree. I felt the blood but it was more like a memory; it wasn't me. I could move and think and see. The world was clearer than it had ever been, but I could

33

not feel my body. I couldn't feel anything. I saw myself obey my instinctive and autonomic commands but I did not experience them. It was like telling someone else what to do and seeing it happen. I was the watcher.

Needless to say, I freaked out. I yelled until my voice turned hoarse. I screamed and cried out to God and Man. Neither one answered. I squirmed and clawed and pounded, like a man buried alive. But all the while I felt nothing and nothing changed. I was in an eternal limbo.

It should have been morning. But nothing had changed. My body, tired from the hours of exertion, began to slow down. I watched it pass out with exhaustion. That's when it occurred to me. That's when I realized that this body was what was keeping me here, in this car. I was so attached to my body that when the connection was severed I did not realize what it meant. All of my efforts were simply an expectation based on memory. My body had stopped responding hours ago. It was my mind, operating based on my mental expectations and limitations of my body that had kept fighting, yelling; trying to live. I can leave; the thought cut through all the fear and trying. I don't have to DO anything. I can just leave.

But where will I go? Fear snatched me back into my body. But I felt nothing in its slumped over figure, only a sense of being trapped. So I took a deep breath that I could not feel and chose OUT. I wasn't sure what it meant. I just chose to be out of the car rather than trapped inside and instantly I was out. There I was on the side of the road when a red Corvette sped by. I saw the red brake lights as the car slowed, then the white reverse lights as it backed up. Great! God has heard my prayer, they saw me. Help is here! I thought. I waved and jumped up and down; at least I thought to do so but the command was met with stillness. My body was back in the car, slumped over the steering wheel. The man in the red Corvette ran right through me. He only saw the me that was in the car. I felt the warmth of his being as he rushed through me to me. He yanked open the driver's door yelling, "Lady, are you all right?!" He felt for a pulse and pulled my lifeless body out of the my shiny new Mercedes. He laid me down gently on the grass next to the tree of my undoing. He dialed 911 and started CPR. I watched him try to revive me and I cried with each breath he forced into my unresponsive lungs. I knew what he was yet to discover. It was too late.

I watched the paramedics put my body into the ambulance and drive away. Loss filled my being and I cried for what seemed like an eternity. I had had so many plans; so much life to live. Faces of my loved ones filled my consciousness. I cried long and bitter tears for the love I'd lost. And still it was twilight on the side of a lonely highway. Time had not moved.

When the tow truck arrived I watched the driver hook up my beautiful new Mercedes with the dent on the side and the blood stains on the steering wheel. He slammed the towing gear in place with no regard for new car. I had picked this baby up from the dealership three days ago after waiting a month for it to arrive. The powder blue paint job and white interior with the sun roof had to be special ordered. As the truck pulled on to the highway with my car in tow I realized I was losing my last connection to my life.

Go. The thought cut through my desolation. And there I was back in the driver's seat of my beautiful powder blue Mercedes Coupe with it's almost perfect white interior. I contemplated the blood stained steering wheel as the tow truck pulled me into the never ending twilight.

The tow truck pulled into a large lot covered with an ocean of cars. He unhooked us and walked away. Now what? I wondered. In the unchanging glow of the faded sunlight I hovered, unsure of what to do, where to go. I sat in the unending silence, waiting, wondering if this were to be my eternity. My life unfolded before me like an

epic 3D saga on a drive in movie screen. Scenes I remembered
clearly and some I knew I must have lived through but had
somehow missed. Did I really say that, act that way, miss that cue?
I watched the endless procession of drama that had been my life.
My family called me bossy, my friends said I was a workaholic,
colleagues called me driven and competitors often referred to me
behind my back as a witch with a "B". Now it all unfolded before
my eyes from their point of view.

Single and forty means fear and loneliness to some. For me it had
meant power. I was the captain of my ship, the master of my
destiny, as the poem goes. I, not some man who couldn't handle
my assertiveness; I, not some snotty nosed kids bleeding me dry of
money and time, determined the course of my life. But as I
watched the unembellished truth I cringed at its harshness. I had
always prided myself on being direct, forthright, no-nonsense. But
now I was privy to the reactions of those I had considered weaker
than myself. In life I was quick to walk away, move on without a
backward glance. I considered it the drama-free life. Now that I
was forced to watch the effects of my every action without the
benefit of my personal interpretation, it was unnerving. I had made
my sweet mother cry, my father sigh. I had left my little sister to
"make it without handouts" and my baby brother to "Man up." All
the while I'd spoken the truth. But I could not be accused of being
kind. I sat in the eternity of my never ending twilight and grieved
for my life. I was no longer grieving for its loss but for its lack of
depth, its sharp edges and stark harshness. I knew now why I was
in my car. It was what had been most important to me; my closest
friend. Maybe this was my eternity.

There would be no second chances, no do-overs, no redeeming acts
in my old age. I shuddered. Then from out of nowhere, anger
bloomed in my heart like a raging inferno. This was not my fault! I
could have changed, given a long life most people reflect and
adjust! But this had been denied me by that Jerk! He had caused
my untimely end. I was fit as a fiddle. I watched my diet and

exercised. My doctor assured me I was in prime heath. It was NOT my time to die! That swerving, Jerk had taken away my chances of redemption. He must pay!

And there I was in the Jazz Club on 79th. street looking into the eyes of the drunken Jerk who had ended my life. The shock of the teleport unnerved me for a moment. He stared at me with sunken eyes that were bloodshot and hazy. "Who the hell are you?" He slurred raising his vodka on the rocks to his lips.
"You can see me?" I was temporarily distracted from thoughts of revenge.
"Of course I can see you! And if you could see yourself you'd clean that damn blood off the side of your head. It's downright creepy!"
"That damn blood on the side of my head," I walk toward him with teeth clenched as I spoke,
"is a result of you running me off the road. You low life Jerk."
The bloodshot hazy eyes suddenly cleared. The Jerk stopped in mid drink, putting the glass back on the table with an unsteady hand. "What the hell are you talking about?" he countered but his voice held the weakness of uncertainty.
"You killed me, you damn Jerk!" I was close enough to smell the vodka on his breath. I would make him pay! I moved closer. "Get away from me you crazy psycho!" He lunged forward swinging his hand across my face in an attempt to push me out of his way. His hand moved through the cool space of my presence touching nothing. The effort left him off balance and he stumbled forward. I stood a step away watching him with deep hatred. He reached for me again. Once again his hands grasped only air.
"What the..?" He turned to me and I could tell he had sobered up quickly.
"I'm dead!" I spat the words at him like daggers and waiting for the effect. He flinched and uncertainty clouded his sobered eyes. "You killed me on highway 66. You side swiped my blue Mercedes in your black Ford Tahoe. I hit a tree and you kept going. Now I am dead and I am here to make you pay."

"You're a crazy Psycho!" His eyes showed confusion but his bravado was loud enough to draw attention to him.

"Sam who are you talking to?" The bartender walked over to him.

"Her!" He pointed at me. "I'm talking to the whack job standing in front of me!" He sneered, emboldened by the audience.

"Who?" The bartender looked at me but didn't see. "There's nobody there, Sam."

"She's right there, two feet in front of you!" The Jerk bellowed.

"I'm telling you Sam, there's nobody there. How many drinks have you had?" The bartender walked through my presence and noticed nothing. He walked off with a final comment. "That's it. I'm cutting you off for the night. No more drinks Sam, I mean it."

Sam, the Jerk, stared at me. I folded my arms as a plan formed in my mind. I may not be able to touch the Jerk but I could make his life a living hell. I smiled a slow and sinister smile with eyes as cold as the body I had lost.

Sam had not always been a Jerk. He'd had a wife and a family. He had played with little hands, kissed little cheeks and tucked them in at night. But that was in a former life. He had not died a physical death. But when the economy tanked and his business failed, he had taken to drinking. His wife, her words falling on deaf ears, had taken their two little children, and had left him. Then the bank foreclosed on their house and he had been forced to file for bankruptcy. He felt as good as dead. The bottle was all that kept him functioning. I didn't know that when I met him. I wouldn't have cared. I knew only hate and it had the face of Sam. I hated him for taking my hopes and dreams, my chances of a future, leaving me in a void of nothingness. I vowed to make the Jerk's life as empty and miserable as mine had become. I had no idea he was already familiar with loss and misery. Mine was a physical death, but he was the walking dead.

I followed the Jerk when he left the bar. To my delight, I found myself able to follow his every move. He could see me and hear me, but no one else could. He climbed into his dented truck yelling obscenities at me. I looked at the damaged bumper covered with blue paint from my Mercedes and rage filled my being. Without a thought I was in the cab, sitting beside him as he pulled out of the parking lot. "Leave me the hell alone!" He yelled. I stared at him through narrowed eyes, "Hell is where we are going." I hissed.

The Jerk drove wildly, swerving the truck and gunning the gas pedal as if he could dislodge my presence with recklessness. He drove like a maniac into the twilight. Once again I sensed a freedom inherent in death. I had nothing to lose. I was already dead. I watched him without fear.

He eventually pulled the truck into a seedy looking motel on the outskirts of town. The poorly worded marquee advertised low rates for long term stays. The large florescent arrow meant to point out the ramshackle building sputtered and shivered as if it were ashamed of its partnership.

He pulled catty corner into a parking space and threw the truck in park. He jumped out of the vehicle leaving the keys in the ignition as he rushed to one of the poorly lit corridors. I was right beside him. He hunted in his pocket until he found the door key, swearing all the while like a seasoned sailor. In the twilight curtains moved and doors opened as other guests looked for a reason for the commotion. They saw only a frantic man apparently maddened by alcholol as he fumbled to open his door. He pushed the door open, squeezed his sagging frame through it and quickly slammed it shut. On the inside of the door he sighed heavily with relief until his eyes accustomed to the darkness and he saw me standing in front of him.

"Jesus Christ!" he yelled.

"You should have called on Him before you left me to die!" I countered. His mad dash through town had only solidified my intent. The haunting had begun.

Throughout his night Sam knew no peace. When he tried to leave I was in front of the door. When he tried to sleep I was at the foot of the bed. When he stepped into the tiny bathroom I was there. Time must have passed for him because I saw that stubble had grown on his face as his sleep deprived eyes looked out of the window. For me it was still twilight. I had watched him skitter and cower as I blocked his every exit. He had exhausted himself with cursing and finally slumped in a dingy old chair by the window. What fight he still had in him slowly ebbed away. I began to grow bored.

Days must have passed in the land of the living. The Jerk, exhausted by his own resistance, fell into a deep sleep. No longer limited by time or space, I watched his dreams, darting in and out of them at will. He lurched with fear each time I did. But as I watched I saw he had deeper pain than anything I could cause him. I watch him reach for little children who slowly faded away. I watched him bury his head in the braids of a woman who turned to aches at his touch. And I watched him cry.

When he awakened he was as ashen as a ghost and I wondered which one of us was more dead. He paced back and forth in the small room, lost in his sorrow. He ate sparingly from opened packets of chips and stale honey buns. The passage of time was marked by the daily knock of a woman half-heartedly offering housekeeping. He refused the service but traded out used towels and asked for bars of soap. Without the benefit of his closest companion, Smirnoff, Sam slowly began to sober up completely.

" I have nothing left to lose." His statement interrupted my levitation. I had spent the last few days exploring the new definition of movement that death had afforded me.
"What does that mean?"
I was curious despite myself. Three days, three lifetimes or however long we had been holed up in the musty room had defused my anger despite myself. Watching his dreams each night had broken through my self-righteousness; compassion nibbled at my hate. This man had once had a life worth living. He had loved and laughed and given of himself magnanimously. I could not say

the same about my own life.

"They are gone. I might as well be dead." He stared through me, seeing not me, but the ghosts of a life lost to misfortune. "I'm sorry I hit your car. I'm sorry I k..." He swallowed hard unable to voice the gravity of his sin. Finally he whispered "I'm sorry I caused your death." He hung his head as he held his hands clasped between his knees. The sign of his penitence stirred the heart I'd never claimed.

"I was a good man once," he was lost in his reverie, "I had a wife, Sadie, and two little girls..." again his voice broke. He fiddled with a worn photograph from an otherwise empty wallet, dog eared and dingy. A faded driver's license fell, seemingly from nowhere, and landed at my feet. It sported a picture of a younger, apparently happier Sam. The address below his picture read, 879 Green Acorn Court. The address seemed to glow in the twilight.
When he spoke again it was like steady rain on parched earth of his soul, "I was a top builder with my own company. When the market tanked I couldn't build an outhouse. My business dried up and so did my savings." He spoke of his life, his loss and his descent into alcoholism. He talked until I wondered who was the captive and who was the haunted. His story kept me bound even as it erased my reasons for binding him. I shouldn't be here. This man is already haunted, I thought with shame. That's when I glanced out of the window clouded with dust and noticed a figure hunched over the steering wheel of Sam's Ford Tahoe. "Someone's stealing your truck!" I yelled, rushing to the window like a limited mortal.

Sam rushed to join me, as his truck pulled out of the parking lot, his unshaven, ashen face held disbelief. "Nothing left to lose," he repeated in a flat whisper. His face sagged and his shoulders slumped. He had given up, on everything. Like a flash of lightening on a dark and stormy night I suddenly saw clearly why I had been bound to Sam. It was not about me at all.

The next instant found me back in Sam's truck, sitting beside the anxious thief. "Hello," I bellowed over his consternation. I had learned a few things about my new state of being while haunting Sam. I collected all my energy and like the unknown in a darkened room once the light was switched on, became visible. The miscreant barreling down the road in his new ride was concentrating too hard to hear my first hello. But when I appeared beside him, paler than death with blood crusted on the side of my head, he lost his ever loving mind.

"Who? What the..Where..?"

All his questions jumbled together in an incoherent mess. He had temporarily forgotten the road. The blaring horns of oncoming traffic gave him whiplash as he snatched his head back to the road and swerved, missing the looming semi-truck by a hair. I could see his heart doing double time in his chest as beads of sweat rolled down his neck. He found his voice again and this time his words made sense. "Who are you and where in the blazes did you come from?"

"From the pit of Hell and I'm taking you back with me." I growled. Sam was no fun to haunt but this fool was like putty in my hands. He turned blue with fear. We narrowly missed another semi-truck and by now my prey was shaking, but he collected the filaments of his bravado. "You're not real!" It's the crack! They sold me some bad stuff!" I decided to dispel his doubts. With a thought, I levitated over the hood of the truck, staring at him as he gripped the steering wheel with white knuckles. He let out a scream and violently swerved the vehicle toward the curb. He barely missed a utility pole. This fool would be no good to me dead and Sam would not benefit from a banged up truck so I refrained from any further theatrics for the moment. "Pull over!" I commanded.

Like a chastened puppy before a rolled up newspaper, he complied. He sat without a word, staring ahead into the twilight, trying not to let his teeth chatter. I could get into this haunting thing, I thought with satisfaction. But for right now I had a plan that involved this sweaty little thief.

"This truck belongs to a woman who lives on 879 Green Acorn Court. You will take it to her, now." The confusion in his eyes vied with the fear for supremacy. "I got this truck at the motel."
"Did I ask you any questions? I said, take it to the address. "Now!"
I took my head off my shoulders and thrust the dangling mess of nerves in front of his face. My disembodied head repeated, "NOW."
The truck took off so fast I almost dropped my head on the truck floor. The pitiful thief was gripping the steering wheel like his life depended on it. I sensed the seat beneath me had become wet with more than perspiration. I noted the fool's wet jeans as the source of the sudden moisture and was smug with satisfaction. I chuckled to myself as I put my head back on my body, leaving it backwards for effect.

Green Acorn Court was almost an hour away judging from the clock radio, but in my never ending twilight it was all one timeless moment. When we pulled up in front of the shabby two story duplex the thief swallowed hard, not daring to look at me but obviously in need of more instructions. I thought for a while, allowing him to stew in his fears. "You will tell her that Sam asked you to bring her this truck. Tell her where you found the truck and offer to take her there." I had been so busy with my new haunting I hadn't thought things out clearly. But I needed to push my advantage so I choose brawn over brains. "Go!" I yelled pointing to the door of the townhouse. "And if you come back without her, you will belong to me....Forever!" I whispered the last word in a low hiss. He was out of the truck and at the front door before the truck door slammed shut.

I watched from the truck as a wan looking woman with long braids answered the door, peering through the small opening allowed by the security chain. As I listened I realized I had struck gold. The thief was a first rate con artist. The thought of losing his immortal soul might have inspired him to greater heights because he

43

embellished the story beyond my weak start. He explained how Sam was deathly ill and in need of her help. He introduced himself as Casey, Sam's friend. He explained that Sam did not know it but he had left his friend and had driven to find her on a mission of mercy. Sadie's pupils grew in alarm at the thought of her husband being in danger. But common sense dictated that she not risk the safety of herself and her children. I knew I had to do something to convince her, fast. The picture! I thought. I willed myself back to motel room where Sam was staring in a catatonic gaze out the window. He blinked when he saw me. "I need this," I snatched the picture he was holding in his hand and before surprise could register on his face I was at the door of the duplex. "Give her this as proof." I told the failing fool, stuffing the picture into his shirt pocket. He stared at me, then at the woman with the braids. It registered in his mind that she could not hear or see me. He recovered himself and pulled out the picture. "He told me if anything ever happened to him I should find you and give you this." He handed her the soiled photograph. That did it. She broke down and wept. It did not take much more effort to convince her. She called to an older woman who she charged with keeping the children and she got into the truck.

When we reached the parking lot of the motel I could see that Sam's room was in darkness. Despite my twilight, I knew this because the surrounding rooms were lit and his was not. Fearing the worst, I teleported myself into the room. Sam was lying face down on the carpet. "Great! His wife will see him passed out drunk," I thought.
"Get up Sam! I yelled." He did not respond. At least I fervently wished he was drunk and not dead. I had some tricks up my sleeve but being in two places at once was not one of them. I doubled back and led our new found friend, Casey who in turn led Sadie, to the door of Sam's room. All the while I prayed that Sam would at least get up before they knocked on the door. Once they made it to the door I rushed through the door. Sam had not moved. The knock sounded at the door. It was time for drastic measures. I

summoned all my energy and raised Sam's prone body from the floor. He levitated above the carpet like a scene from a magician's trick. The instant change startled him into awareness. He looked down at the carpet some six feet under him and yelped in fright.

"Now that I have your attention, listen up!" I was having fun but there wasn't time to relish my new found powers. "Your wife is outside the door. This may be your last chance to get your life back together. So straighten up, and answer the door!" He looked thoroughly confused. His depressed sleep had dulled his sharpness, but at least he wasn't drunk. The knock sounded again and he looked from the carpet to the door, still levitating face down. "Then put me down!" he growled. I obliged. He hit the floor like a sack of flour. I hadn't had time to finesse my skills. "Damn!" Sam yelped. Apparently embarrassed by his helplessness he quickly hopped up from the floor and headed to the door. He regained his bravado in an angry question addressed to the other side of the door.

"Who is it?!"
"It's Sadie." Her voice was a timid whisper from another world. Sam swallowed hard and instinctively started straightening his shirt. "Just a minute!" He rushed to the bathroom, grabbing a clean shirt in his dash. He splashed water on his face and swiped deodorant under his arms, making it back to the door in record time. He paused to heave in a great gulp of air before reaching for the door knob.

And there stood the love of his life; her braids hanging down her back and her eyes anxiously searching his face. He stood looking at her, twitching in anxious anticipation. "Go ahead, hold her!" I prodded. It didn't take much. He grabbed her in a bear hug and smothered her with kisses. "I have missed you so much", he muttered between kisses. Casey and I watched with fascination for Sadie's response. When her arms came up around his neck and she sobbed his name we both sighed with relief.

And just like that I was gone. The walls of the motel room disappeared as I tumbled through space and time. I was in a body again. The awareness came through pain. My head pounded, my throat and mouth were dry. Strange sounds penetrated the fog of pain. I slowly opened dry sticky eyes. The first thing I noticed was that it was no longer twilight. It was morning; sunlight was streaming through a double paned window. I tried to move. Nothing happened. I heard a groan come out of my own throat. My vision cleared and I realized I was in a hospital room attached to an assortment of tubes. Before I could process what was happening my mother's face loomed in my line of vision.

"She's awake! She's awake!" She shrieked until my father appeared beside her. His face was drawn but his sallow eyes lit up with amazement.

A nurse came striding in the room with a reprimand on her lips, "You only have to press the buzzer once..." Her voice trailed off as she followed my parents' gaze. She solemnly reached for the telephone beside my head, then spoke into the receiver, "Get the doctor, she just came out of the coma."

Dying to Live

Leaving the realm of self,
Death you are but Healing's own Womb,
Darkness that Brings The Dawn.

46

Twilight

The Twilight of not knowing;
An endless purgatory until we surrender to
the Joy of not knowing.

The luminescence of Fear

They lie waiting in the dark,
the fears of my life hide
Holding captive my limitlessness
Eclipsing my joys.
But I seek them now.
I seek the dark
luminescent treasures
revealing me to myself.

Deadly Invitations

Hey Death, I don't mean no disrespect
But you ain't welcome here, I don't like your type
Even though I moan and swear and gripe

Sure I've been tempted!
My own life I've resented
But don't creep in here unwanted!
There's a big crop o' hope I've planted
And your boney fingers can't feed my dreams
Your darkness won't add rice to my beans

You thought I called you when I swore I'd die "if"...
The reason has left me but you musta caught a whiff.

Bring the Dawn

But don't get excited, I'm through living in fear
I'll take all those "Ifs" and kick them in the rear!
On my worst day I'll swallow my pride
Hell will freeze over before I give you a free ride!

You thought I called you when I cursed my luck
and called my life a bunch of muck
Life is a struggle and it causes me pain
But there's lotsa living calling my name.
I choose to stay here and live.
I don't care for the alternative.

You thought I called you when I gave up on hoping,
started lying, eating, stealing and doping.
I called your name when I said,
'I wished I were dead.'
But I was talking out of my head.
I'm sane now and I choose life instead.

You thought I called you when I sat out my chance,
Didn't try to better myself or advance.
But don't take that as a welcome mat.
Keep on your coat, take up your hat.
I'm coming out swinging, I'm calling the shots
Life's for the living and I'm giving it all I got.

Suicide

An empty pill bottle beside lifeless fingers
A discharged gun next to a cold corpse
Still waters swallowing the final breath.
People think of suicide as that final act
and so it is.
But most of us commit the petit morte
little acts of death daily
prostrating ourselves before
the false gods of expectations and desire
killing our souls one act at a time.

Patterns

Spiraling in the patterns of our demise
we plunge toward our own undoing.

Soul Ties - Modern Day Vampires

There are some people who live by siphoning off your life
They, kindly or unkindly, require your soul for their presence
They smile and they laugh, they engage your heart
but it's a trap for your soul, your spirit cannot soar.
They live only as you die
and quietly steal only what is of deep value to your soul.
And you, tethered to them by fear or love
weakened by the loss of essential nutrients
cannot find the strength to break free
unless you give up everything you hold unto
and dive into the darkness of your own soul.

49

We Know

He speaks through the wind as it rustles through the trees
She whispers through intuition guiding with an unseen hand
It enters through the senses, awareness bringing presence
Not knowing how we know, we know that we know
And this knowing is what we seek.
It is the roadmap, the light, the force that shows us
We are One, with the illusive but Ever Present God.

This Side Of Death

Nobody's come back to say,
"Whatever you do, don't come this way!"
The Departed are quiet about their role
Quiet and peaceful, is what I'm told.
They keep a secret there's no hurry to learn
Nobody wants it to be their turn.

Mystery cloaked in darkness
Unknowing leads to dread.
But what if it's a return to
From whence we came?
Shedding the body to pass through the veil?
What if the ignorance keeps us in pain
When a loved one moves to a Higher plain?

Could we look with new eyes
realizing death is ever by our side?
The barren winter turns to prolific spring,
the dead beasts feeds the ground
As do we when it's our turn.
All in a cycle no one can own.

Bring the Dawn

If we cannot honor death
though he walks among us strong
Can we see beyond his often cruel hand?
Could those taken be better off
Though our hearts are broken and our minds in pain
Because they have changed form and will live again?

Seeds

Dreams are seeds of life
Buried in the soil of the heart
They grow with tender care.

<u>The Rescuers</u>

Chantilly slowly and carefully peeled both sides of the hamburger bun away from her the patty then carefully licked the mayonnaise off each piece. She ripped the bun into bite sized pieces and added the pieces to the plastic bag of crumbled bread she kept inside her oversized purse. This exercise had taken some time so by now each of the other three people at the table were looking at her with expressions ranging from mild curiosity to disgust. Satisfied with the completion of her process, she looked up from her task to catch the stares. "What?" She asked innocently.

"What's with the bread?" ReAnna asked. Her words were slow and a bit garbled due to a speech impediment but no one at the table seemed to have any trouble understanding her.

"Don't even ask," Sue piped in.

"Oh, that's for the ducks at Lake Ella. I feed them every day. Sassy and Slim just had babies so they need extra nourishment." The stares did not abate.

"You named the ducks? Joe asked but before he could answer ReAnna fired off another question.

"Why don't you just get some old bread from the bread outlet store on Southside?"

"Because of just that, it's old bread. Would you like someone to feed you old, stale bread?" ReAnna shook her head in disbelief as Sue piped in,

"Don't you read the signs at the lake? It says clearly, 'DON'T feed the ducks.' Those signs are posted all around the area."

"Well I can't read so it must not apply to me." Chantilly was squeezing a cup full of ketchup onto her already soggy French fries. She ate them with keen enjoyment, oblivious of the furrowed brows and the looks being exchanged around her.

It was true. Chantilly Taylor could not read much beyond her own name and some basic safety signs. But if you listened to her she couldn't do a lot of things most people thought were important. Yet here she was at 29, still living on her own and doing fine.

The four friends were part of a job club which met every Thursday at Manny's Eatery. The group was born of a social integration project funded by the local vocational department. It had been determined by some higher ups in the organization that people on the fringes of society had a harder time keeping a job if they did not have a social network which included others employed in the same field. Since ReAnna, Joe and Sue had gone through the same job training program and were hired by the same company, they had been assigned to the same employment support group. Attendance was a mandatory part of remaining in the program with its benefits.

ReAnna benefited from the subsidized daycare for her three children. Joe received free bus passes which he treated like gold since they gave him a way to get around.

Sue worked as a clerk's aide in the corporate office. She lived in a two bedroom subsidized handicap accessible apartment with Chantilly.

Chantilly did not receive services from the agency had somehow managed to qualify for the housing stipend. She had taken it upon herself to join the group. She rebuffed attempts by social workers to help her. Years ago she had found a job on her own at a local grocery store as a food bagger. She was now one of their veteran employees. She also collected cans which she recycled for small additional income. No one quite understood how she managed without the wrap around services her friends received from the state program. But they admired her fierce independence and innate ability to land on her feet.

Joe, the most reclusive of the group also lived with a roommate, Tom. Although Tom worked at the same company as Joe he joined the four friends only periodically. He had his own circle of friends at a local day program where he attended part time.

Joe was a table busser in the company's cafeteria and was a
constant source of wonder to Pete, his boss. When the vocational
agency had sent Joe over, Pete, who was the cafeteria supervisor,
had tried to hire Joe as a waiter. He had given Joe a simulated test
to see how he would handle taking food orders. Jane, the cook had
stood behind the counter in plain sight while Pete pretended to be a
customer ordering meals. "Hey Joe, I need you to take my order
exactly as I say it and tell Jane to cook it. Here goes: I need one
hamburger with everything and one plain hot dog."
"Okay." Joe had answered happily. He turned to Jane and informed
her,
"We need two ham and cheese sandwiches and two chili dogs"
Jane had looked over at Pete as if to say what am I supposed to do?
Pete had tried to correct Joe. "Joe that's not what I told you. I said
one hamburger with everything and one plain hot dog."
"That's what I just said," Joe had insisted.
No matter how many times they gave him an order or how they
simplified it, Joe would change the contents of the meal. In the end
they gave him a job clearing away the dishes once people had left.
They had to point out to him that he must wait until the patrons had
left the table because as soon as he understood that his job was to
clear and clean the tables he started clearing away meals while
some of the patrons were still eating. But once he learned to wait
even Pete had to admit they had never had a more efficient or
trustworthy table busser. Joe brought every tip left on the table
faithfully to the wait staff who had served the patron and never left
a crumb of food from the previous meal. He would place clean
silverware lined up so exactly that the tables looked as if they were
in the pattern of a grid.

Tom was the polar opposite of his friend. He possessed an eidetic
memory that made him excellent at recording the patrons' orders
but that brought its own problems. It turned out that although Tom
was long on accuracy he was short on social graces. He never
failed to remind his companions of the exact day and minute

events had occurred and often when they had been wrong or inconsistent.

Despite being very capable, Tom was denied a job next to his friend at the cafeteria. It turned out his accuracy with its attendant honesty was too much for the patrons. He had worked one week of lunch shifts. At the end of the week Pete was on the verge of pulling out his few remaining hairs. He had had over a dozen complaints from irate patrons. Tom had managed to remind his customers of their inconsistencies with alarming accuracy. Unable to abide an incorrect statement he had inserted himself into conversations, correcting the patrons as they held private discussions. One patron, thoroughly annoyed at being corrected, had fired back,

"What are you some sort of idiot savant?"

"Well, an idiot savant is defined as a mentally handicapped person with brilliance in a specific area especially involving memory so that is a reasonable assumption," Tom had responded, "I may be an idiot savant since I am always correct about the facts but since you are incorrect I believe that simply makes you, an idiot." Tom had delivered his pronouncement in his characteristic robotic voice. The staccato cadence of his words added the finality of truth to the silence as he stopped speaking and stared at the man.

The patron had turned a bright shade of red and Pete had been called in to save the situation. In the end a free meal had placated the man, but just barely. Later the same week while in the middle of serving an elderly couple Tom had stopped to corrected the young man at a nearby table who he overheard telling his date that she was the first person he had taken to this spot. Tom had paused in his delivery of the elderly couple's meal to correct the young man, reminding him that he had been in a few days before with a different young woman who had ordered the tuna on rye. The young man had insisted that he was mistaken at which point Tom supplied irrefutable evidence, including describing the clothing the young man was wearing and the name of the young woman he had been courting. All the while the hungry couple next to him sat aghast. The current young woman had stormed out, the hungry couple waiting for their food had stormed out behind her and the would-be Casanova had refused to pay for his meal or that of his lost conquest.

Pete figured he would be bankrupt if he allowed Tom to work another day so he had suggested Tom return to the day program until a more appropriate position, maybe in the records room, opened up. Tom took it in stride. He had returned to the day program but came in each afternoon for a slice of coconut pie with milk until his friend was done with his shift. Fortunately, the storage and retention department needed a filing clerk. There, among a complex system of company files Tom found a haven and a purpose for his incredibly accurate memory. Within weeks he became the "go-to guy" for finding and cataloguing items.

How Joe and Tom became such inseparable friends was a mystery no one could decipher. They squabbled endlessly about who had said this or done that but never did their disagreements carry over into the next activity or the next day. They rolled along like a tumultuous river, spluttering with waves and foam but still flowing as one body in one unified direction.

On a rainy Thursday afternoon in January all five friends met at Manny's. The little restaurant was crowded with people waiting for a break in the downpour. The restaurant was a left over diner from the fifties with its shotgun layout and large glass windows and was dwarfed by its large parking lot. Many a corporation and large business owner had coveted the spot which was at the corner of a major intersection. But Manny's location guaranteed its survival. There was an old two story motel across the street which supplied a steady, if somewhat questionable stream of patrons. The food tended to be greasy or overcooked but people were always popping in for a quick meal due to the convenience of the location. For those who wanted to rest for the hustle and bustle outside the large glass windows made it easy to sit and watch the cars come and go and the pedestrians scurry back and forth at the corner crosswalk. So many people ducked in from the rain that night that the jingle of the door failed to the attract attention of anyone but Tom. He

watched silently as a man in his mid-thirties, wearing a faded black T-shirt and torn jeans dragged and shoved a young woman who was obviously resistant. There was a long pencil thin scar on the man's right
cheek that stood out under his grey baseball cap. The woman also wore a baseball cap along with a tattered red T-shirt with faded writing and a pair of jeans that looked like they belonged to someone twice her size. The man had pushed the young woman into a booth then wedged himself in beside her. Tom watched with mild curiosity as the woman kept her head down and refused to respond to her companion or to the waitress. The man seemed beside himself with anger as he pushed one of the plates of food he had ordered up to the woman's chest. The woman's hair was styled in a disheveled ponytail that hung out of the back of the baseball cap and Tom felt a jolt go through him as the man reached behind her head and jerked the ponytail viciously bringing her features into full view in his attempt to get her to eat the food placed in front of her. Despite her wan pale appearance it was obvious that she was refusing to eat.

ReAnna brought Tom's attention back to the conversation by reminding him that it was impolite to stare. When they walked out of the restaurant toward the bus stop an hour later the skies had clear but Tom's countenance had not. He had still not spoken a word. ReAnna had not missed the uncharacteristic silence.
"What is going on with you, Tom?" She stared at him intently in the gathering darkness. "You haven't spoken a word since you saw that couple in the restaurant. Do you know them?"
"Yes...No."
Now all four friends turned to stare at Tom. He was never indecisive when it came to his memory.
"I don't know them but I've seen that woman before... on television."
"You mean like a movie star? Chantilly asked
"No. She's a missing person. Her picture was on the 10 o'clock news on November 23rd. last year. The day before Joe burnt our

Thanksgiving turkey" Joe started to protest but Sue interrupted. "You mean you think you saw a real live missing person?" She was immediately transported by the drama of it all. "Wow, we could go to the cops and report it and be on TV and get the reward money and get famous..."

"Get a hold of yourself!" ReAnna snapped, "Tom! Are you sure?" That was a ridiculous question of course. Though they often protested, they all knew Tom's memory was the final word on such questions.

"Yes. Her name is Amber Smith. She is 23 years old and was wearing a blue sweater with white stripes in the picture on television. They said she had been last seen shopping in the mall the day before she disappeared. Her family was offering a reward for information leading to her return."

"How much reward?" Sue's eyes were glistening like the raindrops still clinging to trees.

ReAnna ignored her, "It's a pity you don't know where they went." "No, I don't but the man wore a faded black T-shirt, jeans and a grey baseball cap. He had a long scar on his right cheek. They left two plates of food untouched on the table and drove off in a white Ford F150 with a large dent in the tailgate, license # XL973."

Again the friends stared at him in wonder. Tom added, "I was looking through the window when they left. He was pushing her pretty hard and I didn't know what else to do but read the tag." ReAnna voiced what they were all thinking, "You never cease to amaze me man."

"Doesn't that mean we can get reward money?" Sue was determined to hold on to her hope.

Chantilly had been quiet but she piped in, "We can rescue her." "We don't even know where they went. It is a job for the police." "Yes we do, there's the truck, right there!" She pointed to the motel across the street. Sure enough, an old white Ford F150 with a dented tailgate sat parked in front of a row of rooms. They couldn't make out the license plate from there but before ReAnna could point that out Joe was already headed across the street. Cerebral palsy affected Joe's gait significantly, especially when he tried to run but that didn't stop him. He was already half way across the street before the others could react.

"Joe!" ReAnna yelled in a harsh whisper. But it was too late, Chantilly had dashed across the street after him. She was slow of mind but fleet of foot. She caught up with Joe then matched his pace. Sue followed suite powering her electric wheelchair into top speed and so in a matter of seconds Tom and ReAnna were alone at the bus stop wondering what to do.

"I guess we better go after them before they do something stupid." ReAnna sighed.

"It's too late for that." Tom said.

He watched as his friends approached the truck and stared at the license plate. Sue, the best reader of the three, looked back at Tom and ReAnna and gave a thumbs-up.

"Well then we better get over there." Tom was hesitant, "That man looked really dangerous."

ReAnna pulled out her cell phone. "You call 911 and tell them what you know. I'm going after them."

Before Tom could protest she had shoved her cell phone into his hand and was making her way across the street. He looked at the phone for a long moment. He had never done anything so bold and a part of him said no one would believe him. He knew what he had to say was true but in his experience people didn't like hearing the truth, especially not from someone who looked and sounded like him. But as he looked up at his four friends sneaking around the old truck he realized the urgency of the situation. He had to act quickly. His fingers shook as he dialed the number.

"911. What is your emergency?"

He took a deep breath and began his explanation.

Across the street ReAnna had corralled the others into a tight group a few feet away from the truck.

"What on earth are you planning to do?"

"We are going to find out what room they're in and not let them leave until the cops arrive." Chantilly said.

ReAnna, ever the practical one looked at the long two story motel building. She figured there must be about 24 rooms, twelve on each floor.

"How do you think you will know where they are? You can bet they didn't check in under her name. And even if you could figure that out, how the blazes do you figure you could stop them from leaving?"

"Most people don't like to walk. They park close to their room so it's got to be one of these rooms right in front of us. Chantilly sounded confident.

"Or on the second floor..." Sue added doubtfully. Their impulsive bravado began to flag.

"I know! We could knock on each door and pretend to be room service!" Chantilly offered.

ReAnna was not impressed "Room service, in a dump like this?"

"Maintenance!" added Sue.

"That's more like it. But what are we going to do when they open the door?"

"We can stall them until the police arrive."

"Stall them how?" ReAnna asked but once again the friends had taken off, this time toward the hotel rooms.

"You guys stay back and stop them, I'll be maintenance." Chantilly instructed as they walked.

"No, I'll be maintenance. Maintenance people are always men." Joe insisted.

"Okay, say you are there to fix the A/C. My friend Shayla works here and she said the A/C units are always breaking. We will stay back and grab them if they try to leave." Joe nodded and stepped into the dim light in front of the door directly across from the dented truck.

So with this half- baked plan they began their search for the fugitive kidnapper and his victim.

"Maintenance!" Joe said banging timidly on the door. When no one answered he cleared his throat and banged louder. A half dressed man cracked the door slight and looked at Joe through sleepy eyes. "I didn't call for no maintenance."

"Well I have a work order for the toilet." Joe said.

The sleep cleared from the man's eyes as he looked Joe over with suspicion.

"Wrong room." He slammed the door so suddenly Joe almost jumped out of his skin.

No one answered the next door or the next. One man opened the door, took one look at Joe and slammed the door before he could get a word out.

"Room Service!" Joe yelled as he knocked on the next door. A woman yelled "Go away!" without opening the door. Under ReAnna's guidance his friends had retreated to the far side of the truck to wait for the anticipated escape attempt. Finally he reached the last door on the first floor.

"Delivery!" Joe yelled banging loudly on the door.

The door opened so suddenly the suction almost propelled Joe into the room. His mouth went dry as he steadied himself and looked up into the scarred face of the kidnapper. "Where is the pizza?"

The kidnapper glared at Joe through hardened eyes. Fear gripped Joe's windpipe. His mouth moved but no words came out.

"I said, where the hell is my pizza?!"

Joe's voice might have been paralyzed but his feet found their purpose. He backed up and took off in a full blown run. But his unsteady gait was no match for the kidnapper who wanted answers. He caught up with Joe in five quick strides and held him by the throat. "Who are you?"

"A/C repair!" Joe yelled desperately.

"What?" The kidnapper was thoroughly confused. He surmised that Joe could be no threat as his disability was obvious. But that did not explain why he had knocked on his door or what had happened to his pizza. Before he could decide on a course of action the room door opened fully and a girl ran by him at full speed. He dropped Joe like a cat discarding a mouse and dashed after the girl. She was screaming for all she was worth as she ran past his truck in the parking lot. The kidnapper closed in on her, switchblade drawn and glinting in the street light. As his hand grasped the back of Amber's shirt there was the sound of ripping material mingled

61

with screams. Suddenly the kidnapper was swearing and screaming. Amber looked around to see her captor on the ground writhing with pain. Sue had plowed her motorized wheelchair headlong into him and had stopped the chair on top of his right foot. Amber's eyes looked like a wounded animal in the night. She didn't understand what had happened but didn't stop to find out. She took off, her torn T-shirt flapping off one shoulder.

"Stop! Stop! You are safe! We got him!" ReAnna was behind Amber trying to slow her down but she was half way across the street.

"Stop! You are safe!" Amber paid no head but kept running blindly into oncoming traffic.

Tom, seeing the oncoming disaster step off the side walk waving his arms and yelling at the oncoming cars.

"Stop! STOP!!"

Cars came to a screeching halt and swearing could be heard as motorists laid on their horns.

In the midst of the commotion the flashing red and blue lights of a police cruiser forced its way to where the terrified young woman now stood. There was traffic at a standstill on both sides of her and Tom standing in front of her.

"You are safe." Tom kept telling her.

Two weeks later the five friends sat at Manny's Eatery still glowing from their recent fame. Amber had been returned to her loved ones. They had been interviewed by the local news and there were pictures of them all over social media. The reward from the family had been modest and the five friends had decided to donate the money to the local homeless shelter.

"Maybe we should form our own detective agency," Sue said dreamily.

"Or a maintenance company." Joe said

"What?" Chantilly asked

"He means that would be our cover," Tom explained.

"No one would expect it. What people see as our disabilities will be our cover." Chantilly said warming to the idea.

ReAnna rolled her eyes and shaking her head in disbelief took another bite of her tuna avocado pita.

Labels

In the 'disabled'
we touch the inadequacies that belong to us all
and find they do not define one's worth.
In the 'mentally ill'
we see the insanity that stalks us all
And find the hope of resilience.
In the 'children'
we remember our hopes and dreams
and the joys of simplicity.
And in 'the aged' we sense the path to follow
where not to step and when to surrender.
But in seeing each person
In the uniqueness of their being
Is to lose the labels and the judgments and discover
the riches that make us one.

An Elephant Knows

Hi! I am Sam, I live with my sister.
Who are you?
Do you like elephants?
I love elephants because they never forget
And because they are kind and gentle
even though they are huge.
My sister took me to see the circus once
Have you ever been to a circus?
I saw an elephant do tricks,
he picked up his trainer by his trunk.
I got to sit on his back.
I have the picture,
You want to see it?
See me right there?
It was my 30th birthday,
I told the elephant
so he would remember how old I was forever.
I forget things sometimes.
I forget to tie my shoes
I forget my address
I forget to look before I cross the street
Yesterday I forgot my lunch box on the bus.
My teacher gave me a peanut butter sandwich
I love peanut butter.
Do you like peanut butter?
No?
Well do you like tuna?
That's my next favorite.
No??
How about pimento cheese?
No???!
Everybody loves pimento cheese.
Haha! You sure are weird!

.

I Can't Breathe

*I can't breathe
Can you?
bleeding, gagging, bound so you can stand your ground.
My teenage son is dead,
Beautiful black promise denied.*

*While you debate my state and parse the points
I can't breathe!
Can you?
My brother, husband, son's been shot down.*

*I can't breathe
Because air is life and you are crushing my rights!
I can't breathe,
Because breath is about space, a place without judgment.
I can't breathe,
Because you say I stole, I hit, I fight, I'm not right
And before I can defend, you decide my life should end.
I can't breathe.*

Parade

*Fear parading as love
will flood your life with doing,
exhausting efforts of foam and no substance.*

Gaza Strip

I don't know whose fault it is
when men raise arms against their fellow man.
I don't know who is right or who is wrong
Who should leave or who should stand.
But what I do know is this:
Every life is a holy gift
Every child, a sacred trust.
Peace is every man's right
Joy, their Divine portion.
And until we ALL agree
With the right of every man to Be
There will be no peace or joy for you or me.

Bitter Loaf

The bread served here is bitter
still we sit together long hours consuming crumbs
for our true need is that sense of belonging.

The Illusion of Duality

To live in the midst of strife, grief, drama, love
Knowing in the pain that we belong,
Or to walk alone in peace with no affirmation
That is the question.

<u>Sink or Swim</u>

"Take Nagahori Tsurumi-ryokuchi train line to Tsurumi-ryokuchi green line...." Natasha continued on but all I heard after that was "Blahdi Blah Blah Blah." I was looking at the thousands of people rushing by, even occasionally brushing by me as they made their way to the various trains in the underground maze that was the Japanese subway system. In my hand I held a tiny ticket inscribed in ancient hieroglyphics. Sure, it was actually written in Japanese, but what was the difference to me? I couldn't read it any more than I could jump over the moon. But a suspicion began to take root in my mind. We had been walking peacefully toward the turnstile when Natasha and her husband had suddenly stopped. They spoke to each other in Japanese while I tried to hold on to their slippery two year-old. Natasha had then turned to me and calmly informed me, without preamble, that we were parting at this spot. I would be responsible for taking the toddler and finding my way to a football game which would begin promptly in two hour, after which I was to take a second set of train rides to a barbecue at a sports complex. "Huh?! Football game? You mean American football? Barbecue? Today? In Osaka?" I asked. She had looked at me as if she had made the most normal request. Yep. This child was trying to lose me. Sure, my conclusion seemed illogical. The woman standing in front of me was my very own first born daughter. And she had invited me to accompany her and her husband Takeshi on a visit to her in-laws in Nara, Japan. We had just flown over 7,000 miles together from Florida to Osaka. Why would she then try to sacrifice me to the darkness in the bowels of the Japanese earth?

But the root of fear is not reasonable so it quickly grows tentacles which it attaches to logic and reason to keep itself in place. This is a test of my intelligence, I reasoned. It had been less than two days since we had arrived in Japan and so far I had had trouble remembering the most basic Japanese phrases. It didn't help that I had actually visited the country years before. And to my shame I had not studied the list of key phrases I myself had requested she translate for me. So now she was trying shock therapy by suddenly informing me that I would have to find my way to a football field somewhere in Osaka by myself.

"What if I get lost?" My voice sounded whiny to my own ears. Natasha just stared at me, her beautiful big eyes showing exasperation. "Mom, you have traveled all over the world by yourself. How did you find your way?"
"I did so through planning. I did not get plopped in a subway system serving two million people per day on my second day in a country and suddenly have to find an obscure location with no map, no translator and no phone number to call for help!" I fired back, just knowing I had made a clear and convincing argument. But Natasha looked at me long and hard as if she had just discovered that her mother was retarded.

Yep, she was trying to lose me.

Speaking of tentacles attached to logic, my mind quickly switched back to the day before. That was less than 24 hours after we landed in the country. And that was the first time my daughter tried to lose me in this city of six million people.
There we were, standing in the middle of Namba Parks, a giant indoor shopping area amid a sea of humanity when Natasha suddenly announced that I was to find the train station and take the subway back to Nara by myself. I looked at this young woman, formally considered one of my closest relatives and wondered if she had suddenly decided to abandon me or had taken leave of her senses. She pointed in the direction of the subway but I found myself looking at every one of those six million souls streaming by me.
"Which way?" I had asked.
"Mom, the subway is right over there!" She had pointed in a direction I was sure she just made up off the top of her head. That was the first time I asked for a map. "You can get one when you get to the subway."

"I already checked. They don't have one in English!" I fired back. In the end I won that argument since all the subway maps were in Japanese but by then the seed of suspicion had been fully ensconced in my brain.

Now less than 24 hours later they were trying to lose me again. My little granddaughter, unfamiliar with fear, was trying her best to break free and lose herself in the crowd. Hanging on to this bundle of energy grounded me and returned me to sanity. This was not some plot. I would after all be responsible for their only child. I needed to negotiate my way to safety.

I realized the panicked voice was not helping my case so I resorted to the mature adult approach.

"You do realize that when I go missing your child will also be lost somewhere in Osaka, right?"

Natasha rolled her eyes at me but I could tell I was making headway. "Give me a map, in English and clear instructions and I will find you. But ambushing me with your plan at the last minute is a sure way to create chaos. I don't learn well in a state of panic!" I'd like to think my reasoning did the trick but I think they just realized they may actually lose their baby due to her incompetent grandmother. Nonetheless in the end they agreed to have us all ride together to the football field and the sports complex.

Well it may have seemed like I was a fat, fearful chicken but it turned out I was a wise old hen. We had no trouble finding the football field. We watched the interesting mix of cultures. Japanese men suited up in American football gear bowed to each other, Japanese cheerleaders encouraged the spectators to support their team by dancing to American pop songs. In addition to the cheerleaders on the field there was a young woman in the stands passing out cheering equipment and encouraging us to cheer with vigor. At the end of the game the teams bowed to each other and the young woman collected the cheering equipment from the audience. Kirin Ichiban, Japanese beer and American soda bottles were properly discarded and the spectators left the stands almost as clean as they found them. It was time for the barbecue.

We caught the trains they had instructed me to figure out by myself but at the end of the route there was no sign of a sports complex. Once we exited the train station, they asked several people but no one they asked knew the location of the sports complex. I held my tongue but was smug with satisfaction as I watched them question people in Japanese and still not find the complex.
Takeshi, totally at home in his motherland and totally male, took control and lead despite having no idea where to go. We found ourselves in a Japanese taxi heading to where he assumed the complex was located. It turned out his friends had given him vague and somewhat inaccurate information. I sat in the back of the immaculate black taxi admiring the white embroidered seat covers and watching the meter add up an alarming amount of charges in Japanese yen as we circled the area repeatedly looking for the sports complex.

Ironically it was the wise old hen that saved the day. My gut told me this was all wrong so while Takeshi and the taxi driver tried to figure out the vague directions I googled sports complexes in Osaka based on the sparse details they knew. I showed my search to my son-in-law and with this information he was able to direct the taxi driver to the complex. The taxi driver, a patient and mature man, significantly discounted our ride and wished us well.

We joined Takeshi's friends for the Yakiniku, a Japanese styled barbecue. Each table of six people had their own table top grills. We each selected our share of raw fish, steak and vegetables and took turns grilling our own food. Large containers of a Japanese styled sauce were provided for dipping. While the adults enjoyed freshly grilled food and beer the children ate sparingly preferring to play in the grassy area.

There was no acknowledgment that their rash sink-or-swim form of geographical acclimation had actually backfired but when time

70

came for us to return home Natasha and Takeshi patiently accompanied us to our stop before going off on their own. My granddaughter and I happily waved them on. The wise old hen and the little chick had found our way home.

Announcements

Chubby little fingers rip the lever off the new toy
The announcement is made with joy!
"I broke it!"

The little fingers smash the lever back in place
The joyful news is building.
"I pix it!!"

Now the toy is sailing through the air, smashing against the floor.
The announcements peak.
"I drop it!!!"

The joy is complete.

71

Uh-Oh

She is so cute,
Uh-oh!
No!
Stop that.
Catch those glasses!
Save the cat!!
Clean up that spill
Get her off the window sill!
Holy Mackerel! Is she ever still?

Not Quite Two

What would you do,
If you were not quite two and everyone adored you?
Would you sit in your high chair straight and tall
Or would you sling noodles and throw your doll?

If you were the object of everyone's affection
Would you be good, or create a distraction?
Would you put up your toys one by one
Or bite the dog and watch him run?

There is no fun in being cute
Unless you can wreak havoc
And look innocent to boot.

Weather God

Dada sigh,
and fog rolls by
Daddy is up to something;
cloudy skies, wind, haze
Dad says rest;
rain and snow keep me inside
Father is angry;
lightening, hail, blizzard, typhoon and hurricane.

Sunshine and breezy clouds,
Pop smiles again.

Remembering

Gather those scraps of bygone times
when we laughed and sighed
when we loved and cried
yes, and even when we died.

Even the times we hated and perseverated
become precious pieces in the quilt
we weave to cover us in our old age
the cloak of our oneness we cling to
even as we near the grave.

That cloak, that cover, that shroud
becoming a light hearted train of rejoicing
when we gather remembering our where and how
examining each gem-like memory in the Now.

Growing Old

*Each trip around the sun
I chafe and tug against gravity
This grounding stone,
this albatross that keeps me tied to dirt.
I wrinkle and sag,
bogged down by weights of body, mind and soul
But all I want is to soar.*

Miss Jim

*I want my memories back fully and in tact
My grandmother teaching me nursery rhymes
In a bar stocked full of rum and wines,
what were the words, what were the lines?*

*What were those words she bade me remember
while eggs, fried yam and dumplings cooled,
Me drooling for my breakfast before I left for school?*

*What were the gems she shared
Seeming to pull them out of the air?
Where did she hide that strength
That caused her never to show fear?*

*Who taught her the stories she told?
Old Teige and other sad tales?
They are in my memory but access I lack
I want my memories back, fully and intact.*

I Remember

I remember my mother's French roll;
a beautiful golden brown coil of pressed hair,
all strands perfectly in place;
and the little dark brown spot on her left ear
where she had burnt herself with the straightening comb.
She found it difficult to reach the left side of her head
and always managed to nick herself on the ear
with the steaming hot comb coming straight off the stove.
I often stared at that French roll and the price for its exquisite
sheen as she stooped to tie my shoes laces.
But her hands were the mystery of my universe.
Small and almond brown with strong short nails
the soft pink of the sun's first rays.
Her hands would move with such quiet speed and accuracy
that they left me amazed.

Right over left or left over right?
The mystery of tying my laces was lost on me
but those hands held the mystery that tied up all my cares
in neat packages that spoke safety to my soul.
Those same sure firm hands on my back as she zipped up my dress
They scrubbed me clean with a zeal I did not feel,
I holding on to the faucet so as not to slip
and be washed away with the suds,
while they were sloughed off and rinsed down
the racing river of clean.
And I remember sitting at the kitchen counter
watching those same hands creating with mystery and magic
the meal I longed for;
waiting impatiently for those hands to stop stirring
and appear before me with the steaming treat;
the meal I longed to eat
that was safety and security to my young soul.

75

If I Could

If I could, I would hold the beauty of your love
for all the world to see,
This beauty that has formed and raised me, if I could.
I would stay close to you in the endless space called Now,
Stopping the forces of time and holding you close as mine
There would be no tears and no goodbyes.
I would never make you cry and your joys would never die,
If I could.

If I could take your pain,
and like the rain, renew you with every shower
Growing your dreams, fulfilling your hopes,
redeeming them with power
I would surround you with the love you've given me
warming your heart and setting you free,
if I could.
I would give you every day you cared for me,
wipe every tear you shed for me
Give you the life you gave to me,
If I Could.

If I could live the wisdom you've given me,
Show the promise you've seen in me,
there'd be no end to you through me.
Your tenderness, your faithful care,
your love for me that's oh so much
I would give back to you in every touch,
if I could.
And when it's time to say goodbye
on that Shore that final time
I would take your place and go instead,
leaving the very best behind,
If I could.

A Piece Of The Pie

"How much?"

The Rastaman's green eyes glistened as Moyra reached for the carved walking stick. She looked away from the richness of the mahogany wood to find him watching her intently. Quickly she averted her eyes, embarrassed by the intensity of his stare. She looked instead at his cocoa brown skin carelessly covered by an ill-fitting faded blue jersey. It was adorned with random holes from the dint of circumstance rather than the choice of fashion. His khaki pants had fared better than his shirt, covering his lower half with dignity all the way down to his worn leather sandals. By the time he opened his mouth to reply she had re-clothed him in a grey Armani suit and placed him on the cover of Island Times Magazine.

"What's it worth to you?"

His cryptic reply jerked her out of her reverie and left her wondering if this was the strategic move of a seasoned negotiator or the careless floundering of a poor businessman.

She hefted the carved wood. It was two inches in diameter and three and a half feet in length with a carved handle. The wood undulated with notches every few inches. This gave it a wavy appearance but when she put its base on the ground it felt firm, balanced and strong. The mahogany of the wood changed hues throughout the length of the piece giving it a subtle but rich iridescence. If the rod was a natural beauty, the handle was truly a work of art. It was made of ebony inlaid with mother- of- pearl chips that looked cool but felt warm to her touch. When she gripped it, she had the sense that it belonged in her hand for a purpose, not unlike the wheel of her Mercedes, her favorite carving knife or her fountain pen; a finely honed weapon.

"Well it's just a stick, like a dozen others in this market. So I guess I'll give you $5 US." She met his eyes with her best negotiator's stare. The Rastaman's eyes didn't waver. In fact his stare intensified, burning a hole in her conscience.

"You get what you pay for. This is no ordinary rod. This is a replica of an ancient rod filled with mystic power. If you want a $5 stick there are plenty around. If you want this rod, offer me a fair price." The green in his eyes darkened to a piercing jade.
Am I being censured by a market vendor? Offense mushroomed in Moyra's mind. She stuck the walking stick back in its bin, turned on her heels and strode off. *How dare he?*

Cairo, Lebanon, Madrid, Istanbul, she had bargained with the best all over the world. How dare he imply she did not recognize quality? She would buy another one just like it within view of his stall so he could feel the sting of losing a sale. As if an extension of her thought, a voice rang out,
"Ma'am, would you like to buy this lovely wood carving? It would look great in your house! Makes a nice gift for your friend!"
But even before she could stop she could see that these carvings were inferior in quality. She kept walking.
"No? It's on sale today! An extra special price for you!! Ma'am! I'm talking to you!!!" "As Moyra kept going, ignoring the sales pitch, the heckler turned nasty. "Who you tink you is? You walk like you have two left foot! Go'way! You don't deserve mi carving!"

She wasn't thin-skinned. You couldn't be a good journalist and not have a hardened hide. And Moyra was one of the best in her field. The two Pulitzers back home in her New York apartment attested to that fact. As she walked the craft market she calmed down enough to question her sudden, uncharacteristic anger. Why had she reacted so impulsively? Her assignment, indeed her entire career required a calm demeanor. But this entire island culture unnerved her. Everywhere she went the natives found a reason to yell "No problem man!" like it was a national refrain. The happy go lucky, no hurry attitude annoyed her intensely. Something was wrong, there was always a problem, if you dig deep enough you could always find the root of a problem. Her career as an investigative journalist was predicated on that premise. Her Type

A personality drove her to find that problem. And there was definitely a problem on this sunny, happy little island. What's more, that Rastaman with his fake mysticism was a link to the whole rotten mess.

By the time she circled the craft park on foot for the second time she realized with chagrin that the Rastaman was right about one thing. There was not another stick like the one in his stall in the entire market. She could still feel the strange pull of the smooth cool wood with its vibrantly warm handle. *I'll be darned if I give him the satisfaction of going back and buying it*, she thought. So she headed out of the market. The green eyed Rastaman was packing up his stall when she walked by on her way to the exit. At a glance, there was no way of knowing if the stick had been sold. He glanced at her with disinterested eyes as she walked by, turning to pick up his collection of hemp sandals.

Why was he leaving so early? It was mid-afternoon and all the other vendors were showing no sign of leaving. This may be the link she sought. She quickly selected one of the more reliable looking local taxis cabs waiting outside the market and determined to engage his services exclusively. She jumped into the front passenger seat and handed him a US $20 bill. A quick introduction told her his name was Exton and that he was available for any journey on the island with the $20 deposit. He insisted on renegotiating the fare if the journey took more than two hours. He took a bite of the flaky yellow patty inside the soft white coco-bread he held in the small brown paper bag; then quickly tried to recover the crumbs that shower his chest. A quick swig of yellow liquid from his fizzy bottle of D&G pineapple soda and Exton was ready to go.

I have news for you buddy. That $20 is all you're getting from me, Moyra thought to herself as she watched him eat with relish. But aloud she was more diplomatic.

"We'll see. I'll tell you where we're going in a minute," she said watching the Rastaman pack up his raggedy, rusted burgundy 1982 Toyota Tundra pickup truck.

Before long they were following the Toyota Tundra up into the hills of Jamaica. Moyra's last ten days on the island had been leading to this very moment, a breakthrough in her story on the illegal Jamaican marijuana export trade. Sure, marijuana and Jamaica were synonymous in a lot of peoples' minds. But Moyra knew in her gut that the group she was tracking was different. This group had been quietly moving high quality weed directly into the hands of some powerful people in the US. There was a sophistication and precision about their movements that suggested a deeper story. Her sources indicated that governors of a few border states, some members of congress and even the presidential front runner for the upcoming elections were involved. She intended to get to the heart of it. If her instincts were right (and they'd never been wrong yet) this story would earn her next Pulitzer. She'd been focusing on Mr. Emerald Eyes for the last five days. His striking features as well as his patterns of behavior had caused her to single him out of the crowd of market vendors. He never heckled like the other vendors did, he seemed very nonchalant about selling his wares and he always left earlier than the others. His stall saw more than its fair share of foot traffic. In fact more locals ducked in and lingered in the little space than tourists. This hit Moyra's radar immediately. This guy was no common market vendor. She would bet her next pay check he was a part of the marijuana group she was searching for and if her luck held she would have proof by the end of the day.

Moyra was feeling pretty smug about her progress until the taxi jackknifed and Exton threw his standard shift Toyota Corolla into fifth gear.
"What...??!!"
She glared over at the driver letting her expression communicate her dissatisfaction.
Exton was unapologetic.
"Yuh want mi to follow dis guy or what?"
She had been so lost in her reverie she had not noticed the change

in terrain or the fact that the Toyota Tundra had suddenly increased speed, putting several car lengths between them.

"Do you think he suspects we are following him?" Moyra asked. *Maybe we were too close behind for too long*, she thought. She chided herself for having lost focus.

"Naah man. Is so we drive in Jamaica. Everything cool man."

But it wasn't cool at all. Moyra had been on the island long enough to know that driving in Jamaica was a hair raising, death defying dash up and down the mountains and that these taxi drivers were confirmed fatalists. It was like watching the Indy 500 except the roads were only wide enough for one vehicle and you were a captive in the front passenger seat with the other cars, trucks and busses coming directly at you.

The exciting thing about the Indy 500 is the understanding that your favorite driver is as committed to living as you are. But these Jamaican taxi drivers showed a cavalier disregard for death. Exton beeped his horn and passed a weighted down dump truck around a hairpin curve. Moyra swallowed hard, clutching the "Oh God" handle to avoid landing in Exton's lap. As her life flashed before her eyes her journalistic mind calmly registered that driving with a fatalist has its disadvantages. If he fully accepts death as an imminent possibility and you are a passenger in the car, your choices might be severely limited. As the unhappy passenger watching the winding road racing toward her, Moyra reflected that fate appeared to have conspired to make her an unwilling partner in her driver's date with death.

But her threat of death would be realized from a far different source. Exton was in fact an expert driver. He followed the Toyota Tundra off the main road and unto bumpy dirt paths ascending one hill after another for what seemed like hours. The landscape became more magnificent as they penetrated the interior of the island. Finally the truck rounded a bend and came to a stop at what appeared to be a random spot in the dirt path it was using as a road.

81

Exton, expert in driving but not in undercover work, was taken by surprise at the sudden stop. He down shifted his Corolla in time to come to a stop three feet behind the Tundra. He and Moyra looked out the windshield into smoldering green eyes. The Rastaman was standing behind his truck, legs apart and arms folded. Moyra and Exton sat very still in the car looking like guilty children caught in a forbidden act. The Rastaman didn't move. Behind him the sun had begun its journey home for the evening casting a glow that surrounded him like an aura. Moyra's instinct propelled her into action even as her gut tightened with fear. She opened the door and stepped out of the car.

"Why you following me?" The Rastaman's words were slow and even but his voice held a rumble like distant thunder. Moyra had not planned on getting caught, so she had not prepared an excuse for her intrusion. Had they been anywhere near civilization as she knew it she could have brushed aside his question saying they were simply taking the same road. But the remoteness of the area left her at a temporary loss for words. Much to her surprise Exton spoke up.

"Wha' appen Dread? De lady here find you interesting, seen? She want to learn about di Rasta culture." That was pretty good, Moyra thought with surprise. She sighed with relief.

"Can you speak for yourself?" He was burning a hole into her with those green eyes.

Moyra recovered her wits and stepped into her journalist role.

"Yes. I'm a U.S. journalist and I'm here to do an article on the Rastafarian culture." It was mostly true, she reasoned.

"Then why didn't you simply ask? Why would you trail me for hours and try to sneak into I and I's castle?" Moyra was confused for a minute. What castle? All she saw was trees, hills and bush. Exton rescued her again.

"He means his home. His castle means his home."

Moyra had researched marijuana and Jamaicans in general, not the Rastafarian language or culture. She knew they used the herb liberally but she was not familiar with the lofty references like "I and I" and "castle". Who did this guy think he was, a king? God?

She swallowed her distaste for his arrogance and took Exton's lead.
She threw out a bait for his ego.

"You see? That's what I'm here to find out. The world wants to
know more about your lifestyle, your castles, how you see life."

"Then read a book. I and I live a private life. Intruders not
welcome." As he spoke the sun dipped behind a hill and a chill ran
through Moyra. She had not thought this out properly. It would be
dark soon. If driving over hills and mountains had been
treacherous, then driving back down in the dark would be suicidal.
An ideal mushroomed.

"I am willing to pay you well to let us spend the night at your...
castle and observe your customs. How about $100 U.S.?"

Exton was shaking his head before the words could fully leave her
lips and when she looked at the Rastaman she knew she had made
another mistake.

"Neither you nor your blood money are welcome here." This time
the thunder in his voice was unmistakeable. He had not moved
from his stance but somehow Moyra got the feeling that he had
pushed her backwards.

Once again Exton intervened, "Dread, I don't know my way back.
It would be safer if we could find a spot to katch until morning."
He spoke matter of factly and after a lenghty pause the Rastaman's
ire subsided.

"Follow me. " He abruptly turned on his heels and got back into his
truck. Moyra and Exton jumped into the car and followed closely
behind. But their relief was short lived. The Rastaman simply
pulled off the dirt path and parked the truck in a copse of trees.
They pulled in beside him, parked and scrambled out to catch up
with him. He was walking rapidly up a rocky trail with a bundle of
what looked like sticks and other items from his shop slung over
his shoulder.

"Are we leaving the vehicles here for the night?" Moyra was out of
breath when she caught up with him.

"The vehicles are safe for the night. The only way to I and I castle
is on foot up this hill." He said the words without breaking stride
or turning around. Moyra and Exton looked back and realized they

couldn't even see the vehicles in the looming dusk. What they could see was that the trail ahead was narrow, steep and treacherous. Exton let out a long sigh. Moyra swallowed hard and threw her camera bag over her shoulder.

"What the hell have I gotten myself into?" She didn't realize she had spoken aloud until Exton gently tapped her on her shoulder offering reassurance.

"It's no problem man, Rasta are good people."

Forty five minutes later Moyra was no longer swatting at mosquitoes or pushing away thorny weeds that sought her flesh through her denim pants. Her bare arms felt like they were on fire from the bites and scratches. But she paid this no heed. She was panting; crawling on her hands and knees up the slippery crack in the latest boulder thinking, *I can't do this any longer!* All her pride in her physical fitness had slid down the last hill they just climbed in this unending ascent. Exton was assisting her from behind as delicately as he could while trying to preserve her dignity. A good shove on the behind would have placed her quickly atop the latest knoll but he was a gentleman. He resorted to more awkward placement of his hands, supporting her shaky legs as she tried to get a grip. The sun had set, leaving only the soft grey of early evening and still the Rastaman walked stoically on as if he were strolling on level ground. Moyra started to hate him with an irrational intensity. When the ground finally leveled off she would have kissed it with gratitude except that the Rastaman quickened his pace and was disappearing into the twilight. Her wooden legs moved clumsily under her as she trotted after him. Exton walked quickly but easily beside her. She started to hate him too.

When lights began to dance in the distance their appearance sparked a glimmer of hope in Moyra that the journey would soon end. Slowly the flirtatious glimmers solidified and she was able to make out a small village ahead. The lights were warm and welcoming but Moyra felt a strangeness about them.

Nearing the compound she began to hear the steady rhythmic drumbeat that had been infusing its' way into her consciousness. Now that her mind had become aware of it she suddenly realized that she had been hearing it for some time as they trudged through the darkness. It was unlike anything she had ever heard before. It was like the heartbeat of the earth beneath her feet.

"What's that sound?" She whispered to Exton.

"It's Nyabinghi."

"Huh?"

"It's Nyabinghi, the sacred music of Rasta."

"Greetings in the name of Jah." Moyra jumped half out of her skin as the deep voice sounded in her left ear. She whipped her head around and stared but still she could not see the village sentinel at his post beside her. Seeing no one made her unsure whether or not to answer so she swallowed the lump of fear and move closer to Exton who replied easily with a,

"Greetings Dread."

"Do you see anybody?" she whispered.

"Naah. Must be a Maroon. Camouflage is their specialty."

A few minutes later they entered the gateway to the village. The entrance was unmistakable even in the darkness for their eyes were aided by a faint glow coming from within the village. There were two large white stone columns, each topped with a life sized statue of a lion wearing a crown on its head and holding a flagpole in its front right paw. Two young Rastas stood guard, one on the inside of each column. They greeted the Rastaman who said something to them that neither Exton nor Moyra could hear. After the brief exchange he continued through the open path between the columns without looking back. They hesitated for just a moment before realizing he meant for them to follow.

Inside the village Moyra's eyes adjusted to the lighting. Slowly the strange glow began to make sense. There was a large open wood fire smoldering in what appeared to be the center of the village. A well-worn path which formed a circle around the open fire. Soft shadows reached her from rustic homes that sat on the outside of the circular path.

A small group was gathered around the open fire. Moyra realized the source of the rhythm that had moved her as the men in the center drummed in ecstasy. The women danced in rhythmic but wild abandon. Without knowing why she was pulled to the group. That was just as well because without warning their green eyed guide cut across her path and took his place among the drummers. The visitors were left to decide how to adjust to their new surroundings.

Exton joined Moyra on the fringes of the group. They sat gratefully on the cool earth watching the drummers. As their eyes adjusted to their new surroundings Moyra realized why she found the lighting so strange. There was no sign of electricity throughout the village.

A soft voice behind them interrupted their thoughts and they turned to find a slender woman wrapped in Kente cloth and a matching scarf that swirled upward to cover a tower of locks. She was accompanied by a young girl who wore a simple long tunic. Both were holding bowls filled with hot steaming food. Moyra was a staunch animal activist and vegetarian but she hadn't eaten since having a lone mango for breakfast. The uphill climb had stripped her of much of her sense of scruples. She would have eaten a raw steak at this point. Fortunately, for her sense of dignity, the bowl was filled with steamed vegetables seasoned with exotic smelling spices. They dug in with relish, both uttering unintentional sighs and groans of appreciation as the delicious meal filled them with satisfaction.

The woman returned as if on cue as they slurped down the last of the stew. Exton, without any apparent sense of embarrassment asked for a second and a third helping. When it was clear even to him that his stomach could hold no more Exton sat back on his heels and surveyed his soundings. The young woman moved so silently that they both jumped when she appeared between them.

She directed them kindly but firmly to separate buildings where she provided them with the basic items they would need to prepare for bed. Moyra peppered her with questions but the only one she would answer was her name. "Call me Imani," was all she said before closing the door of the room. And so it came that Moyra found herself lying close to the ground on a firm, comfortable futon staring into the darkness. What was this place? How did it function? Why was it so far away from civilization? She pondered these questions before her exhausted body refused the tyranny of her mind and she fell into a deep sleep.

Her dreams were dark and labored. She was struggling up another hill. She couldn't get her footing. Her arms flailed wildly as she tried to grasp the tree limbs around her but they grasped back pinning her hands over her head. She was choking as dirt from the hill rolled into her mouth. No, that wasn't dirt. It was a cloth of some kind. The shock brought her fully awake. The limbs holding her were real arms. She had been gagged and tied and was being held firmly by two sets of arms. In the darkness she could see no one, only outlines of bodies. Her scream was a small muffled squeak thanks to the cloth in her mouth. Cold panic struck her mind like lightening in a dark sky. She writhed, stiffened and lunged. All to no avail. The outlines hefted her over their shoulders like a roll of carpet and stepped into the deep darkness of the night.

Back at the village the sun took it's time meandering up the mountain. When Exton emerged from the hut refreshed by a good night's sleep but worried about his lack of a cell phone signal and his dying battery. He was also starving. He followed the enticing aromas hoping to satisfy his growling stomach. Imani had anticipated his needs. She handed him a plate of freshly steamed green callaloo seasoned with onions, peppers, garlic and tomatoes and all thoughts of his useless cell phone faded, at least for now. The vibrant green spinach-like vegetable was surrounded by slices of rich yellow roasted breadfruit. The crispy brown edges around each slice indicated the breadfruit had been fried to perfection. He

was on his second helping when the green eyed Rastaman walked up to him. He held a bunch of freshly cut sugar cane in one hand and a gleaming machete in the other. With one glance Exton knew the Rastaman had been up for hours. It was only seven in the morning but he suddenly felt lazy. "Morning Dread," he muttered. "I and I am called Joshua," without waiting for Exton to acknowledge he went on, "where is the American?" Exton looked sheepish. He had been so caught up in the delicious meal he hadn't even thought about his passenger. "Still asleep?" he guessed. "No, the bed is empty." This came from Imani. The Rasta dropped his supplies and headed for the small house where Moyra had slept. He emerged less than a minute later.
"She has been kidnapped," his words were carried to Exton on the wind because he had already retrieved his machete and was heading into the bush.

The endless night of fear left Moyra wired like a malfunctioning electrical circuit. She had not slept a wink. Her hip and shoulder hurt from been unceremoniously dumped unto a hard floor in the corner of what appeared to be a hut. All night she could hear the voices of men and smell the tell-tale aroma of marijuana coming from outside the hut. Their voices waxed and waned until the moon rested its head on the crest of the hill. She could not understand most of what they were saying. They spoke in heavily accented Jamaican patois and the effect of the ganja seemed to confuse their speech. Only one thing became clear to her. She had found the group that was responsible for the large systematic exports of marijuana. Or rather, they had found her. She grimaced at the irony of having found the source for her story at the possible loss of her life. When the sun's rays touched her bound body through the only window in the hut her mind struggled to find in it a thread of hope. The thread snapped when a short, heavily muscled man walked through the door with a keenly sharpened knife. He snatched the dirty rag out of her mouth and asked "You been snooping around. What you want? Who sen' you?"
She shook her head to try to understand more clearly but he took it

as a refusal. "So you not gwine talk? Then you will pay wid your life!"

"No! I mean yes!" I'm a journalist. I'm doing a story on the marijuana trade." The words tumbled out causing her parched throat to burn.

He laughed harshly, "You Americans tink you can police de world! For de last 50 years uhnu persecute, kill and lock us up for selling weed. All of a sudden it legal in yuh country but uhnu still want to control de trade!"

Moyra did some quick translations in her mind based on her experience and figured that "uhnu" must mean "you". He was suggesting that she/ Americans didn't want Jamaicans to profit from the now legal sale of cannabis.

"No! That's not it. I'm not trying to stop anything. I'm just trying to tell the story."

"Liar!" he spat at her. With a violent jerk of his arm he raised the knife. Terror seized Moyra. Her eyes squeezed shut and her body tensed as he slashed downward. She thrashed and screamed as she felt the knife rip through the flesh of her left thigh. She screamed in agony as another swing of the knife landed it in her left shoulder. Her eyes flew open unable to stop herself from trying to see where the next knife strike would land. His arm was swung high above his head. Moyra's chest ached to be shielded but she could not protect herself. In that split second of anticipation she felt the beat of her heart and the blood rushing through her veins. Then everything froze. The man's hand remained above his head, his body paused in mid action, his face frozen in a grotesque contortion of hate and shock.

The next minute he was on the ground and the Rastaman was standing over him holding the blade that still dripped of Moyra's blood. She blinked at the surreal scene, too shocked to comprehend the rescue. He reached for the ropes that bound her and in a minute she was free. She lay there shaking, too afraid to be grateful. "Let's go," was all he said. When she didn't respond he unceremoniously picked her up and draped her over his left shoulder, her behind facing forward. He headed out the door and into the bush. There was no sign of the men she had heard throughout the night. She didn't have time to wonder. The Rastaman moved through the bush with rapid agility. Various tree limbs and leaves slapped Moyra in the face as they moved through the dense foliage. The morning mist still clung to the leaves, rudely delivering to her face and throat the moisture she had longed for throughout the night.

When they entered the clearing of the Rasta Village all was calm. Unlike the wild thumping of her heart, everyone moved at a slow and rhythmic pace. It was still early and the children were wiping sleep out of their eyes as their mothers set about their chores. Joshua left Moyra in the care of the women and headed off at a brisk pace. She wasn't sure how long she slept but she was aware of a poultice on her thigh and the ministrations of women.

The sun was playing hide and seek with the trees when she opened her eyes to see Exton sitting beside her. "You lucky to be alive," he said softly.
"Why me....?" Moyra's questions could not fully take form. Exton understood and explained. She had been kidnapped by another sect of Rastas who thought she was a spy of some kind. They had come into the village unnoticed because they were neighbors and often traded goods. This Rasta sect was heavily involved in the growing and exportation of marijuana and was positioning itself to take advantage of the opening American market of legal medicinal marijuana. Their stance in the export trade had put them at odds with several other groups and the tensions had led to paranoia.
"Joshua blames himself for what happened to you," Exton said in conclusion.
"Who is Joshua?"
"The Rastaman who brought us here. The one who rescued you from the Kingman village up the road," He gestured as he spoke pointing in the direction of the neighbouring village. "the one who just saved your life. He feels that because he brought you without letting everyone know who you are it put you at risk. He and the

elders had a meeting. They are talking to the men who kidnapped
you right now."

Moyra digested the information slowly. "They tried to kill me,
what is there to say?"

"He is negotiating your safe passage back to the city." The gravity
of her situation settled in her empty stomach like a rock. She still
wasn't safe.

Exton seemed to read her mind, "Don't worry man. Joshua has
skills. You safe now."

Moyra sighed, turning her head toward the door as Imani walked in
with a steaming plate of bright yellow ackee, golden brown
plantains and wheat flour dumplings. Exton, having already had
two helpings threw his head back and laughed in delight. "Don't
worry man," he repeated "after you eat that ackee you will feel that
all is right with the world!" *How could such a small man be so
obsessed with food?* Moyra wondered but she took the plate and
dug in. The tastes of the island rose up to greet her in every bite.
Things started looking up. Exton was right.

Time was a dense soup of dreams as Moyra rested to regain her
strength. She had lost a lot of blood during the mad dash through
the bush. Her left side felt like a broken wooden plank had
replaced her limbs. But as she recovered so did her curiosity. Now
that she was not in danger of imminent death the journalist in her
had been reawakened. Who were these guys in the bush? Why
were they willing to kill her if their dealings had been legalized?
How could such a ragtag group carry out such systematic
distributions with such precision and how were they able to
connect with the Miami, New York and Chicago drug lords? What
was their connection with leading US politicians? She knew she
was only on the fringes of discovery. She had to find the money
trail to find the real power behind the operation. She had to return
to the scene of her intended demise. She had to find that hut.

So at 5:00 a.m. before the first rooster cleared his throat to
summon the day, Moyra rolled unto her fully functional right side,

dressed herself through gritted teeth and slipped, or rather limped, out of the door of the house. The morning had not yet awakened but the glow from the central fire pit guided her in the direction that Exton had pointed. As she crossed the courtyard with its smoldering fire, the pain in her left side began to command her attention. She wouldn't get very far with this painful limp. Looking around her she saw what appeared to be a shed. She pushed aside the unlocked door and hopped inside as quickly as her battered body would allow. She breathed a sigh of wonder as her eyes grew accustomed to the light and she discovered that she was inside a storage area for some of the most beautiful wood carvings she had ever seen. *This is not the time for admiration!* she told herself. She focused on finding a stick that would serve as a crutch. The light of the fire reflected off the handle of a stick causing her to notice it. It glowed like a magic wand in the darkness. She reached into the bin and pulled out the very rod she had been admiring in the craft park. It would serve as a good walking stick, she reasoned.

As she gripped the rod a surge of power shot through her arm and into the rest of her body like lightening across the dark sky. The pain in her limbs no longer registered. She felt almost giddy with energy. Swinging the stick before her she literally sprinted out of the hut and into the bush.
She could not explain it but she knew where she was going. She dismissed the feeling that the stick was leading her. She abhorred superstition.
When she came upon the clearing with the hut where she had been captured she marveled at the coincidence that she had found the place. Some of the same voices that now haunted her dreams could be heard floating across the pre-dawn light. Four men were seated around a small card table engaged in a game of dominoes between puffs of joints that left fat clouds of smoke above their heads.

She peered through the bushes trying so hard to understand what was being said that she froze in shock when a hand grabbed her shoulder. It was Joshua and even in the semi darkness she could see his scowl of disapproval. He reached down to grab the rod from her as another hand from behind knocked him forward unto the ground. In a flash Joshua rolled unto his back and knocked the legs out from under his assailant and they were tumbling in a violent bundle of fists, elbows and knees. The man who was twice Joshua's weight and several inches taller managed to pin him to the ground in a choke hold.

"The rod!" Joshua croaked with his right arm flailing toward Moyra. She had watched the scramble not quite sure what to do. Even with the increased light from the rising sun she could not clearly distinguish who was who.

"The rod!" Joshua croaked again as his body thrashed wildly in his assailant's grasp. Moyra thrust the rod at his flailing hand. To her surprise it leapt as if under its own power into Joshua's hand. As his fingers grasped it, it began to glow. Joshua simply rolled to his left dislodging the larger man with new found strength. The stunned attacker found himself beneath the smaller man, unable to move. Joshua stood up pointing the rod at the man who still found it impossible to move.

"Come!" His voice was low but urgent as he glanced over at Moyra. She scrambled to her feet and attempted to sprint after him. Without the rod her pains had returned. Still holding the rod he turned toward her and grabbed her by her arm. Again there was that flash of electrical energy she had felt in the shed. It seemed to travel from the rod through Joshua and into her. She didn't believe that was possible but the jolt was unmistakable. "What is that thing?" she marveled looking incredulous.

"No time for questions. We have to fix the mess you made by coming here." Joshua walked quickly dragging her along with him. When Moyra realized they were heading straight for the hut of her undoing she began to panic and tried to pull away.

"No!" She screamed but it was too late. The domino players were at full attention, spliffs held at bay with smoke curling around their arms.

"Why you bring this woman back here?!" The question was barked at Joshua by the man closest to them. Moyra recognized the voice

93

and her blood receded from her veins. He was the one who had tried to kill her.

"Tell Bigga we here to speak with him."

Moyra's would-be-killer jumped to the task, apparently anxious to be out of Joshua's reach. He rushed around the back of hut and that's when Moyra noticed a larger wooden structure on wood pilings behind the hut. The man quickly disappeared inside the darkened building.

Bigga, the local leader of the group, did not take kindly to the early morning interruption. He could be heard swearing loudly when his man informed him that he was being summoned. When he emerged from his doorway Moyra saw a large shirtless man behind what looked like an enormous beer belly. His face sported a sour countenance but once he saw Joshua, for reasons unknown to Moyra, he held his peace.

"Wha' happen Dread? Why you come so early in the morning and bring dis woman. I thought we had an agreement."

Before Joshua could respond Moyra jumped in with the tenacity that had earned her her first Pulitzer. "Your men kidnapped and tried to kill me. The least you could do is give me an explanation."

"Woman, me don't owe you Jack!" Bigga's countenance quickly turned from sour to stormy.

"What the lady mean is that if you have a legal operation why can't you give her an interview." Joshua's tone was easy; his words sounding like a reasonable request.

Bigga's face showed a range of weather changes as he considered Joshua's words. It finally settled on partly cloudy. "Alright, I have nuttin' to hide, " he threw his head over his shoulder and yelled suddenly, "Ferdie! Put on some Blue Mountain coffee and bring me a spliff!" Then he grabbed the chair formerly occupied by Ferdie who had so rudely awakened him and motioned to the other men to give up their seats to Joshua and Moyra. They scrambled up and stepped away from the domino table. When Joshua and Moyra were seated he asked. "What you want to know?"

Moyra sensed the chance of a lifetime. She charted a course of questions starting with the least offensive ones. "With such a profitable and legitimate operation, why are you guys holed up in such a..." She swallowed the world 'dump' before it was uttered, " such an obscure place."

Bigga was no fool. His sudden laughter frightened the chickens that were pecking in the yard behind the hut. It almost unnerved Moyra but she held her ground.

"Woman you are judging from your perspective. This is some of the richest, most fertile land for growing ganja. It is also almost inaccessible except by foot and helicopter. So obscure for us is good. And if you are judging by our humble dwellings..." he waved his hands in a grand stage like gesture at the few building around them, "then you misunderstand the intent of ganja export." Moyra's brows furrowed and Bigga, the consummate showman took center stage to paint the picture of his logic. "These buildings are not our homes, we come here to check on the crops and prepare them for export. My house would put your ordinary American middle class man to shame!" His stuck out his chest and for a moment it almost equaled the size of his belly with the haughtiness of the boast.

Ferdie appeared with a cup of steaming hot liquid. Bigga who was now immersed in his own self-importance shot rapid-fire questions at his underling. "Why you only bring one cup? You don't see we have guests? Where di sugar? Dis betta be Blue Mountain, y'know. I don't drink inferior coffee!"

Ferdie put the cup down among the dominoes and quickly retreated with a series of, "Sorry Boss, yes Boss, coming Boss, yes Boss." A few minutes later three steaming cups of coffee where place haphazardly among the dominoes. She did not want to accept anything from this man but the rich nutty smell of freshly roasted Blue Mountain coffee was seducing Moyra. Bigga was pouring in sugar like his life depended on it. She glanced at Joshua for cues on what to do. He sat stoically watching the sun slowly climb out of its bed of valleys. Bigga followed her gaze and suddenly his face resembled the sun rise around him as realization dawned. "Ferdie! Ferdie! Wha' wrong wid you man! You don't know de Dread don't drink no caffeine. Get him some bush tea! Right now!"

Ferdie could be heard crashing around in the distant kitchen as he hurried to obey the latest request. Moyra's stomach growled. She longed for the coffee with all her soul. Surely a cup wouldn't hurt. She reached for the cup and fiddled with the handle waiting for Joshua to stop her. He continued gazing lazily around him with one hand resting casually on the rod. So she put the cup to her lips. She had experienced good Jamaican coffee in her hotel but this freshly roasted bean took her taste buds by surprise. She literally sighed with pleasure when the taste hit her palate. Both men turned to look at her and she felt the blood rush to her face. "Great coffee," she offered feebly.

"You got that right! Best in the world!" Bigga's braggadocios affirmation allowed her to regain her balance. She picked up her line of questioning.

"Why did you try to kill me?" In the big picture this was a petty question but Moyra was still seething from the attack.

"Naah Man, we wasn't gwine kill you, I just teaching you a lesson, seen?"

Her eyes narrowed. Nothing he said could have convinced her of that so she moved on with her questions.

"What about the moral aspect of selling marijuana?"

Bigga looked confused. Moyra restated her question.

"Do you ever think it's wrong to sell weed?"

"Moral and legal are two different things in this world, you nuh see?" Bigga's eyes narrowed. He laid down his coffee cup and as if for emphasis pulled a spliff from behind his ear and lit it.

"Here's what I think, Nature is my god in the flesh, man. I check say everything come from Nature.

Ganja come from Nature, yuh nuh see? Ganja is a holy weed. Jah is my God and Jah make the weed. Weed don't hurt anybody. It just make people feel good. I wouldn't sell anything that hurt people. But I- Man smoke weed so I make my living selling it."

"As long as De Man wasn't making de money weed was immoral and illegal. Now that they find a way to get paid they want to make it a plantation crop. So they legalize it to take away the immorality. For De Man, money determine morality and legality. But for Rasta there is a Higher Power and Jah control Nature so there was never a discrepancy. If De Man ready to buy then I ready fi sell. I- Man figure it's Rasta time to make a profit." After an hour and a half Moyra had most of the answers she needed. She had figured out that "De Man" was Bigga's way of identifying the establishment, the legal system, the power brokers. "I-Man" was another one of the way Rastas often referred to themselves. These guys weren't the power brokers, she would have to return to the U.S. for that and she had some ideas where to start. The fly in the ointment here was the philosophical rift between Rastas like Joshua who believed the herb was sacred and should not be used as a weapon of commercial exploitation for the profit of a few and those who felt the time had come to cash in on a crop that foreigners had long since benefited from financially while those without connections were still being jailed for possessing a joint. This rift went beyond ideology. Profit was driving this rift and where money was involved things usually got nasty. People were willing to kill or be killed in the fight for their share of the pie. She had almost been a victim of that view point.

She followed Joshua in silence all the way back to the village. A man of few words himself, he recognized that she was deep in thought and said nothing until they entered the gates.

"You need to rest," as he uttered the words Imani appeared at her side and began ushering her to the building she had rested in the day before.

"We leave in the morning."

"Leave?" She was still deep in the matrix of the ganja trade.

"For Ocho Rios. Exton is taking you back to your hotel." He strode off with the rod in hand before she could collect her thoughts and reply.

The walk back to the vehicles was no easier for being a decline. Pain flared in Moyra's hip every time she stepped downward unto uneven ground. She determined not to let her anguish show, clenching her teeth silently as she walk with Joshua in front and Exton behind her. Joshua stopped so suddenly she almost ran into him. He turned, handing her the rod in one smooth motion as he did so. She recognized the handle in the gentle morning sunlight and took it gratefully. Once again she felt that surge of power that had propelled her the day before. She had to ask.

"What is in this stick?" her voice had an incredulity that made it clear she was not asking about the obvious physical attributes of the rod. Joshua, who was still facing her, stared right through her. He replied to her query with a question of his own.

"Why do you ask?"

Moyra was left without a parry. She prided herself on empirical evidence and something inside of her told her that there could be no logical explanation for what she felt. Finally she made a weak attempt.

"It feels... I feel.... different... when I hold it." Her words were almost apologetic.

"You feel different," Joshua began and she nodded thinking he had understood her question, "then the question must be asked of you: What is in you?"

Her face flushed and Moyra swallowed hard to abort the sharp tongued response that arose in defense of her status as the one with the riveting, revealing questions. Joshua was still staring at her with those piercing green eyes. Exton had been too far back to hear the full exchange. He moved closer to the two of them wondering what was the reason for the hold up. He was getting anxious to get home and they were a long way from his car.

"What wrong wid de stick?"

For all he knew this was no time to be talking about a walking stick. He stepped up the Moyra and his eyes caught sight of the rod. He stopped in his tracks and fell silent. Moyra noticed the change in his demeanor and now burned with curiosity. But before she could formulate a question based on logic Joshua whirled around and started off in the direction of the vehicles.

"It's getting late, let's go." His words held the finality of a door slamming in Moyra's face.

When Moyra later looked back on that walk down to Exton's car

98

there was a dreamlike quality to the journey. She had felt no pain and could not clearly identify any of the hardships she had encountered on her way up. She tried to excuse this by pointing out to herself that one was an uphill climb, in a strange place in the dark while the other was downhill at the crack of dawn but somehow this simple logic failed to capture the difference she experienced.

One thing she remembered clearly was Joshua's face as they said goodbye at the bush were Exton's car remained hidden. The sun had risen high enough to stream through the trees behind him making his locks appear to glow and blend in with the sunlight. For a timeless moment she could say nothing, taking in the ethereal glow that surrounded the moment. Exton broke the spell with the sheer practicality of his impatience. Now that his cell phone could once again receive a signal he had scores of missed calls and over a dozen messages. He had a lot of explaining to do and the anxiety drove him outside of his usual 'no problem' attitude.

"We need to go. It's a long ride back to Ochi."

Moyra's head was throbbing from the weight of the as yet unformulated questions she longed to ask. And her heart was struggling with emotions she could not identify. She felt she was losing something she could never again touch when Exton ushered her into the front passenger seat of the Toyota Corolla but she could not justify standing there trying to figure out what to say. Before Exton closed the door she pointed the rod at Joshua pushing it toward him in her gesture. He held his hand up as if to say stop and she felt the resistance of his gesture as the rod froze suddenly resisting her momentum. Her face held a stupefied look but Exton wasn't having it. He had endured all he could take of strange events. It was time to get back home.

"He wants you to have it' he told Moyra.

Then moving faster than she had ever seen him do, he took the rod out of her hand and gently laid in on the back seat of his car. In a flash he had made it around to the driver's side and was backing the car out from beneath its hiding place in the bushes.

"Take it easy, Dread!" he yelled as he rolled down the window. Joshua gave a slight bow and Moyra watched as he quickly disappeared from view around the first rocky bend.

They drove in silence for a long time. Exton was using every navigational skill he had to find his way back and avoid the pot holes, goats and sheer cliffs prevalent in the countryside. When they finally returned to paved roads Moyra found her voice.

"I can't explain half of what happened to me. I feel like I was in another world where nothing makes sense but it all works out perfectly."

"Of course you were. This is Jamaica." Exton said matter-of-factly. "I just need to convince mi girlfriend of that when she ask me where I been for the last three days."

Jamaican Resilience

The hope that simply will not die
The indefatigable believe that we will succeed
The ingenuity that defies logic
The ready smile and the carefree laugh
That insists "We little but we tallawah!"
That's what it means to be a Jamaican.

Coming Home

What are you doing in Brisbane or Spain,
Mississippi, Idaho or Maine?
Aussie, peseta, green back or shilling,
working, working but not living
Who are your people, what is your name?

Trying, dying, just surviving, growing hardened,
growing old in vain.
Who are your people, what is your name?
Who do you belong to, what keeps you sane?

What are you doing in New York, LA,
Minneapolis, Austin, Spokane?
If nobody loves you, no one knows your name?

I Miss You

I miss your rhythm
I miss your smile
I miss Rahtid, Kuyah! Guhwhey and Soon Come!

I miss the Trade Winds that use to blow through the open windows
toppling off the lamp and breaking the vase;
The cows blocking the country road
And goats stopping traffic at Halfway Tree.

There are beaches here
But I miss you
Caribbean blue.

Hot lobster patties, cold cream soda
and green mountain peaks that take my breath away.

Lavender Lightening

Cumulous clouds in a flash
Lavender lightening dancing in the night sky
Dark ocean waters rushing by

Rooster Response

There is a call and response
in each rooster's crow.
What one says, the other knows.
Each inflection carries a message
telling stories carried by the Trade Winds.

Thunder

Rumble shaking the bowels of earth
Lightening illuminating the sky
Wind moving waves
Trees bowing in homage.

Ancient Longings

Old and New and new and old
ancient longings in place of belonging
Gripped by need, displayed as greed
The history of a lost race,
The face of a broken promise.

Sweet Rain

Sweet rain falling like the tears of God.
Faithfulness in the morning dew
And in the raging hurricane.

Gentle spring rain
Reviving dead and long forgotten dreams
Speaking newness and life
In old and broken places.

Strong summer rain
Touching the hot and feverish earth
Like a mother's hand
Bringing balance to a sun scorched land.

Angry autumn rain
Erasing the illusions of youth
Making room for the nucleus of Truth.

Cold winter rain
Liquid snow washing away regret and all that's old
Opening the floodgates of Heaven
With treasures untold.

Sweet blessed rain
Pouring out deep refreshing
Filling my rivers and my seas
Making me all I hope to be.

Let it rain.
Sweet blessed rain.
Let it rain.

Cloud Series

Something out of Nothing

A cloud forms;
Something out of nothing
Billowy white
Visible yet untouchable
Ethereal splendor

Sky

Sky;
A beautiful nothingness
In which is everything.

Big Bang

God said, "Let there be..."
From the Silence comes the First Sound
And all of Creation manifested.

Raindrops

Counting the raindrops as they fall
Sliding down rooftops, eaves and all.
One million and one
One million and two
Now a river running through.
Soaking the flower bed, the fresh laid sod.
Washing away the willful old
and the passionate new.
Countless raindrops,
rearranging the landscape
bringing change with impunity,
and wild abandon

Presence

Presence
The absence of petty worries.

<u>Wild Women</u>

The check-in line in the lobby of the spa told its own story:
Young adults engrossed in their cell phones, blurred the clear
distinction of the lines by leaning against the walls, while men and
women, still wearing professional attire, stood obediently but
impatiently in front of the check-in staff. Couples with the languor
of vacation leaned into each other seemingly unconcerned about
the wait. Skittish housewives fidgeted as they waited for their
controlling husbands to offer up the credit card that would pre-pay
their stay and leave them to their respite.

It was New Year's Day and I wondered if all of Atlanta had
decided to converge on this one spot. We had driven around the
parking lot several times before settling on a remote parking space.
I had no idea what to expect since, except for the sign, the large
nondescript exterior held no hint of what was inside. When my
girlfriends had invited me to the "spa" in Georgia, I had envisioned
water bubbling up from underground springs into large wading
pools outside a rustic cabin completely surrounded by nature. My
fantasy had been rudely shoved aside by the busy metropolis as we
darted through traffic on the packed interstate highways, hoping to
stay alive long enough to reach our destination. When we exited
the freeway I had held onto my fantasy, expecting us to meander
along a winding country road that headed out of the city and led us
to an obscure spot nestled in the foothills of Georgia. Instead I
found myself staring at a commercial block of buildings. Judging
from the size and shape of the building they identified as the Spa I
had the impression I was stepping into a large warehouse. As we
stood in the cramped little lobby I consciously adjusted my
expectations and was just grateful to be with my friends. We were
given our shorts and shirts and our ID bracelets with a key to our
lockers. We stepped into the changing room filled with rows of
lockers and dozens of women in various stages of undress. I was
ready for this, having experienced a Japanese spa only months
before, naked women did not intimidate me. Obviously everyone
around me was also ready for the experience. No one gave the

other a second glance as women stripped down to bare skin inches from complete strangers. What surprised me this time was the number of people of color all around me. We joke amongst ourselves perpetuating the stereotype that black women don't like group nudity or getting our hair wet. But here I was surrounded by Sisters in the buff freely submerging themselves, hair and all in heated whirlpools.

The spa had three distinct sections, an all-male and an all-female area where each gender could soak in the hot or cold pools, sit in the saunas or receive health and beauty treatments completely nude and a co-ed section where everyone intermingled or lay in the heat of various dry saunas dressed in the spa outfits they received at check-in. We started out in the co-ed section where everyone sported matching spa uniforms. The saunas were shaped like igloos. To my amazement the walls and ceilings of each of the dry saunas or kilns was completely covered, inside and out with healing and semi- precious elements from the earth. There were various stones and crystals including amethyst, jade, salt, charcoal, and other minerals. Outside the door of each sauna was a small sign suggesting the healing benefits that would result from being steamed within those walls.
The only furnishing inside were mats on which to sit or lie as the heat detoxified your body.

We mingled with the men and women who had all come for a common purpose; rejuvenation. And as we did we shared thoughts on food, healing and worship with complete strangers from every background, color and creed.

Before long we made our way into the deeper sanctity of the all-female wing. Shedding our clothing we entered a small traditional hot steam sauna. This was my first encounter with such a contraption. I had never been inside a dry sauna either but those made sense to me. A dry sauna required only the willingness to be hot enough to sweat and the patience to allow one's body to adjust to higher temperatures. To me this was not unlike a hot day with no breeze. If one sat still enough and relaxed the mind you could discover a peace from being still and an appreciation of the sweat that implied the release of toxins.

The hot steam sauna was another matter. My friends were kind and gentle offering me a small bowl of ice and a small towel as I entered the room. I soon found out why. The little rooms could comfortably hold a maximum of six people if everyone sat upright on the wooden bench. The steam made it difficult to even make out the bodies as you entered the room. As I stepped in the wave of hot steam that hit me made my insides lurch like a bad tempered mule being pushed over a cliff. Everything inside of me said, 'Back up and run!' So I halted and took a step back. But the fool that is the logical mind said, "You've never actually tried this. Your aversion is illogical. Look, your friends are calmly and peacefully finding a spot to sit and detoxify. Why are you afraid of a little hot steam? Don't you need to detoxify?" So, led by the fool masquerading as reason, I overrode my instinctive reaction and found a spot to lay my towel and took a seat. Well within five minutes there wasn't enough ice in the bowl or in all the world to cool my heated skin. I vowed at that moment never again to casually eat a lobster who had been dropped, live, into a pot of steaming water. I was that lobster and I wondered if he also cursed the foolish act that had led him to be caught and steamed alive.

My friends were calmly and sweetly meeting new friends and exchanging beauty tips, all while intermittently swabbing themselves with a cool towel from their ice bowl. My ice had quickly turned to a bowl of steaming water. I heard nothing, saw nothing but the Devil himself smiling as he fanned the flames of my personal hell. I bid him a good day, collected my towel and my hot bowl and hastily headed out the door. I heard him laugh as I slammed the door behind me. The whirlpool that had previously felt so hot was a welcome change from Satan's inner sanctum and I checked all my appendages to make sure I had not left any parts of me behind in the steaming vat he called home. I hope for the lobster's sake that it lacks the cognition to perceive its fate, but just in case it does know what is happening when it is lowered into that pot, I once more vowed never to eat it again.

By the time my friends exited the steam room I had regained my composure. We signed up for body scrubs. This time it was my friends who were hesitant, having experienced the merciless vigor of the "aunties" who performed the cleaning. These workers were deceptively small middle aged Asian women who went about their jobs dressed in skimpy, skin tight attire. Their attire had nothing to do with sexuality. They exuded sheer practicality and since getting wet was a part of their job they dressed accordingly. They could be seen through the open archway vigorously pommeling women who lay on massage tables and unceremoniously pouring buckets of water over their bodies. It was not foolish bravery that led me to risk having my skin peeled from my body for a second time. It was the realization that after that steam room with Satan's hot breath on my neck, a small Asian woman with a scrubbing mitt could not intimidate me. Well I was somewhat mistaken.

My friends and I each lay on massage tables covered with surgical grade plastic while the women who appeared to know a total of six words in English instructed us to lie on our backs and relax. They covered our eyes with warm compresses (probably so we wouldn't panic) but I peeped over at my friends on the nearby tables to see what to expect. They had begun their body scrubs a few minutes before me so I watched with morbid fascination for a few moments before I was sternly admonished to close my eyes and surrender. I was left with the image of my friends being slammed around and pounded by older women in their skin tight shorts and tank tops. The image was quickly replaced by that of a Brillo pad as my "auntie" doused me with a pail of warm water and began scrubbing me with a scratchy mitt. She had no regard for my body as an live being of beauty. No, no. This was a toxic sack from which she must remove several layers before she could be satisfied. She scrubbed my legs with maniacal vigor, slinging them around with a lack of concern for damaging their function. The scrubbing mania began to approach more tender places and I began to panic at my naked vulnerability. There were areas on my body that could not survive the onslaught of a scratchy mitt. Fortunately for me, the auntie's single minded purpose was to remove a few layers of toxic dermis from the most obvious and exposed areas. I peeped out from under my eye covering again and saw dark clumps falling off of my body as she worked.

"Is that dirt?!" I asked in horror.

"Dead skin." Her perfunctory answer had no hint of personal interaction. She continued to sling me around with the strength and energy of a woman half her age and twice her size, staying focused on her mission of removing the toxins from the covering on the sack I called a body.

My friends beside me were not faring any better. From time to time we each experienced a sudden dousing of water as our respective aunties washed away the layers they had removed from our skin. But the water was warm and the vigorous scrub was strangely relaxing. It was obvious that this woman was not about to relent in the ferocity of her attack on my skin so I slowly began to surrender and let her return my skin to baby soft purity. When the final bucket of warm water came crashing down on my body she removed the eye covering and said,

"Finish!"

It took me a few seconds to realize that this was not a command for me to do anything, but her way of letting me know the session was over. I tried to thank her for the invigorated feeling that now possessed me but she was not interested in my thanks. She pointed to the shower and ushered me out. If only the lobster had been given this choice he would never have ended up in that steam pot.

We were so refreshed after our scrubs that the vigor with which they were administered instantly became a pleasant memory. We reassembled with glowing skins and sat quietly basking in the stillness of our deep refreshment. My friends are both powerful healers, each in her own distinct way and so as we sat, having

removed some of the layers that cloud who we are, women started
to approach us. We offered prayers and songs and soon a small
group of women we had never met joined us sitting side by side in
a circle. Without plan or instruction we began to minister to the
emotional and spiritual wounds that had driven these women to
seek refreshment. Women wept as prayers were whispered over
them, words of wisdom were spoken and healing songs were sung.
There were the tears of releasing and the laughter of infilling, the
rest of belonging and the peace of being understood. We were an
oasis of healing in the endless desert of obligations. Other women
around us, read quietly, soaked in whirlpools or performed beauty
treatments, each finding their path back to wholeness. The sanctity
of our spontaneous circle of seven women sitting quietly in deep
union went beyond race, culture or creed. We had never met before
that moment but we knew each other with a knowing that was deep
and timeless. In that space we knew our Oneness and from that
place each of us left refreshed and reaffirmed.

Preparing to leave the spa we dressed ourselves and collected our
belonging just as a new group of women entered. It was obvious
from the wide eyed stares and the questions that tumbled from
their lips like unruly children that it was their first time. After
looking around the locker room one woman asked me, where do
we get undressed.
"Right here," I said.
"In front of everybody? Oh no I need some privacy, that's too
much exposure for me!" she insisted. She took her belongings and
headed for the restroom. I smiled, little does she know, I thought,
that the sense of rejuvenation she seeks will come only after she
has exposed her own vulnerabilities.

111

I And The Fire Are One

*I have stopped loaning out my soul
to the taskmasters of the world.
No longer will I do their ego's bidding.
Fear will no longer fracture my intentions
Nor confusion my destination.
No longer will I be a victim of the forgetting
that steals my soul's light.
I and the Fire are One
As I walk the Path I set ablaze.*

Mirror

*I cried to know You
wondering at my sorrow and lack
till looking in the mirror
I saw You staring back.*

World Balance

*She carries the world in her womb,
And on her shoulders.
She rocks the planet in the cradle of her affections
She balances it upon her knees,
Singing it songs of hope and mercy.
She is its guardian and its nurturer.
So when she cries
Something or someone in the world has lost their way,
Or died.*

--

112

Sistahs

We used to hold hands and spin until we fell down,
dizzy and giddy in our oneness
That was many ocean tides ago
when life had not yet succeeded in separating us.
Do you remember?

We used to braid each other's hair
And laugh at the silliness of anyone who was not us
Taking each other's beatings for the sake of loyalty,
Do you remember?

We used to dream of a future where you were queen
And I was your royal advisor until the next day
when I would be queen and you would advise me.
Remember?

And when we had to leave home,
You heading east and I west
We swore an oath in each other's arms
that the miles would never separate us.
Do you remember that?

Now we are grown and carried away by life's cares
Each trudging through the lonely sands of obligation
Each having only memories of a time when we were inseparable.

AI

The ultimate enemy of Humankind
being birthed in the mind of man.
Erasing traces of the Spirit.

Neglect

Flowerpots huddle on the porch
Filled with old soil and lanky weeds
Signifying neglect of my soul

Earth Touch

My sun dappled lawn beacons
I couldn't see it before, blinded by demands...
But now it's Sunday morning, time to restore my soul.

The Blessing

Thank You for the blessing of the impossible
In it is the miraculous.
In it is the humility and the patience of blindness.
trusting where I cannot see and
waiting when I cannot move.

Endless Well

Yearning is an endless well into which
I throw all the longings of my heart
And wait for them to travel the rivers of life
Finally flowing into the ocean of contentment.

Faded Memory

Was it a dream when I laughed with easy joy
carrying a large sack of hope easily about my shoulders?
Did I really run and jump and dance?
Or was I always in this decayed trance,
watching my skin wrinkle and my life rush by, out of reach?
I hoped for love once
and the chance to make a difference in the world,
cavorting on the shores of an imagined life
but reality's waves washed away my dreams
leaving me abandoned on a becalmed sea
Now all I have is a faded memory of the me I had hoped to be.

Soul Command

Soul I command you,
to remember God's kindnesses
This moment, this breath
this fulfillment of a secret desire
this answer to a desperate prayer.

Remember and be glad.
For times will come when
His faithfulness is not so clear
and you will have to hold dear
all the wonder and the love He has shown
and the way He met you here.

So soul, I command you
to remember God's kindnesses
in this moment, in this breath
as He fulfills your every desire

.

Seeing

See action before it's born
Through a door of discipline called awareness
A clear mirror into eternity.

The Biggest Secret

There is no "They"
There's only "us" and "we".

Likewise there is no "I"
that is separate from the whole.
"You" and "Your", "me" and "my"
"us" and "them" are all expressions of a Oneness
that cannot be seen;
All the physical manifestation of Being.

When "They" and "Them", "You" and "your",
"us" and "we" all become "me" and "I"
in the mind and attitude of Man,
"we" will all live in the Ultimate Reality of Being.

Green Sea rolling

Green sea rolling
Waves are trolling
in search of the cares of life
stresses and cares crashing the shores
breaking them against the sands
until they are no more.

Digging deep into the soul
the sea finds the grains of pain
and rolls them into waves
crashing them against the shores of life's realities.

Sweet Songs

Sweet songs of deliverance
echo across the skies
birds and oceans make their cries.

Sweet Seas

Sweet seas of solitude
Fulfilling my dreams
with the ocean's tide
ebbing and flowing yet ever knowing
The answer to my soul's desire.

<u>Cold Bath</u>

I avert my eyes. I don't want to witness my own death. There is no way the oncoming Mercedes SUV can miss hitting our little Ford Focus. The road is barely wide enough for one small car, let alone two. My eyes shut tightly as my entire frame tenses for the impact. Instead, I feel my body suddenly jackknife to the right as our car abruptly cuts across the lane in front of oncoming traffic, missing the SUV and, without pause, continue speeding along a connecting road. I open my eyes to see the scenery has changed. We are no longer on the busy boulevard. There are red brick homes on either side displaying long stemmed roses in tiny front yards.
"Crazy Brits!" I mutter under my breath.
"What's that?" my cousin asks as she barrels down the middle of the lane narrowly avoiding cars parked on both sides. I don't tell her that I think she, and the other millions of drivers on the roads of London are mad. Nor do I reveal my sweaty palms and racing heart. Instead I smile at her sweetly and ask,
"Is the traffic always this... hectic?"
"Oh, this is nothing!" she brushes my concerns away as she zooms over the speed humps at 90 miles an hour. To be fair, her odometer reads in kilometers but 90 is 90 to my alarmed mind. Something tells me the speed humps are meant to reduce speed to a rate sedate enough to see the colors of the roses as they go by. At this point the flowers are a blur. I sigh. American drivers rise up en- mass in my mind like a vista of calm and sanity. I see the wide multi-laned highways and millions of cars all at least an arms-length away from each other like a mirage of a traveler's Utopia. Now I'm going mad, I think, shaking my head to clear it of fantasy. I ask my cousin,
"I guess the road rules here are really just suggestions, huh?"
Before she can answer me she slams on the breaks. The seatbelt keeps me from going through the windscreen.
"I will be glad to see my chiropractor when I get home", I mutter again. Fran lets out a hearty laugh as she punches the gas and makes a hard left.

This has been our daily ritual since I arrived in London five days ago. So it is with some relief that I hop on the subway, or Tube, as it is called in London and find my way to the Victoria Coach Station. I reasoned that taking the subway and the coach tour should provide me with some stress free drive time. I will not have to worry about oncoming traffic, imminent death or whiplash. I will simply enjoy the English countryside when it is visible from train or coach and walk peacefully among its treasures.

"Your guide's name is Rita." The tour company's assistant directs us to a large red coach with expansive glass windows. "Right this way for Bath, Stonehenge and Salisbury." An idyllic day lay ahead of us visiting ancient Roman Baths, Mysterious Stone Structures and amazing architecture.

I meet George and Rita at the coffee shop. We bond immediately in our mutual agreement that a hot cup of coffee is the perfect thing to accompany us on a long bus ride on this cold, wet, dreary day. It has not stopped raining in London for three days and the cold is starting to settle in my bones. We trust that Bath will be sunny but for now we hug our coffee cups like new found treasure. "No drinks on the bus! You will have to toss that coffee." Rita turns out to be a brawny, bald, middle aged man with intent hazel eyes, a large round head and drooping ears like an elephant. His ego is even larger than his ears.
"You!" He points at George. You'll have to throw that away."
George looks at Rita then at his coffee cup in disbelief. "But we just bought..."
Rita doesn't allow him to finish, "Toss it or stay behind," he snaps, dismissing George with a sharp turn toward another passenger who has a question.
This tour will be in English only," he tells the multi-national group. "but I was educated at Oxford. My interest is in ancient Roman studies, so if you insist I will speak Latin." He spouts off several phrases, presumably in Latin with the obvious intent of subduing

his charges into instant meek adoration.

Carol and George are not impressed. They have just dumped two full cups of coffee because of our guide's hubris. It doesn't help that we can see passengers in the other coaches beside us eating and drinking freely as they wait to depart the station.

"He's treating us like second class citizens!" George growls. I glance around quickly thinking tensions are about to flair. But Carol, who has been married to George for almost 50 years, doesn't even look up from her map. Lucky for us Rita is off on a rant about how Shakespeare was wrong about where Julius Caesar was stabbed to death.

"I don't give a rat's ass!" George mutters from behind me. This could get heated, I think for the second time. Carol is still reading her map. Fortunately Rita's voice fills his own ears so he cannot hear George's heckling.

"Great Britain has 68 Million people. We have more Nobel prize winners than any other country in the world. We sell wine to France, sausage to Germany and pasta to Italy! In 1971 the Queen sent the first email. We received the Nobel Prize for the DNA discovery. We have the number two biggest film series ever; Harry Potter AND the number one biggest series; James Bond!" Rita's chest swells as he rattles off his country's honors.

"London burned to the ground in 1666," Rita continues.

"You'd think with all those smarts they'd know not to have the bakeries with their ovens in the center of the town!" This time George's voice is distinctly audible. Rita bristles but the other passengers give a hearty laugh so he refrains from responding and moves on with his list of impressive facts.

By now I have a bigger fact to contend with. I had chugged my coffee, not wanting to waste it. I had ignored the fact that caffeine is a diuretic. We are half an hour into our journey and this fact is starting to make an unmistakable impression on my bladder.

"Does this coach not have a rest room? I ask George and Carol who are seated behind me.

"Nope." Carol says after glancing around.

George offers his refrain, "Second class citizens!"
"How long is the trip to Bath?" Rita is annoyed that I have
interrupted his soliloquy.
"Two to two and a half hours depending on traffic," he snaps
before adding, "Now where was I?"
By the time we get to the Cotswalds I am no longer hearing Rita or
seeing the beauty of the green undulating patches of country side. I
am watching the rain in the distance and the water that is rolling
freely down the large glass windows of the coach. "I'll be wetting
my pants." I decide.
I am so desperate to pee that I reason insanely, "No one will know
since we'll all be wet. I'll just be wet all over."
But we make it to Bath before I am forced to make good on my
decision.

Bath is a beautiful city whose buildings display a predominance of
golden colored bath stone and Georgian architecture.
Rita gives us all radios tuned to a channel where we can hear him,
then he leads us to the entrance of the Roman Baths. As we walked
through the rain he chatters about the caramel colored volcanic
stones that adorned the facades of most of the buildings in Bath.
But all I am thinking was Bath-room!
"You may explore at your leisure. We will meet at 5 minutes
before one," Rita was saying, "and if you are not at this spot you
will have to find your own way back to London for a minimum of
£360."
Right! I think. Who in their right mind would let themselves be
stranded in this weather so far from the city? I run off to the rest
room without hearing the rest of his instructions. Little do I know
that wetting my pants might be the better option at this moment.

The baths are an impressive network of bathing pools originally
built by the Romans using the local hot springs. There are
significant architectural treasures including the remains of the
temple of Sulis Minerva a combination of the Celtic goddess of the
Sun and healing and the Roman goddess of wisdom.

I tour the Roman Baths and marvel at the engineering, the remaining architecture and the artifacts. The head of Sulis Minerva hints at her former glory. The bones of ancient inhabitants tell their own tales. The rich can be identified by the erosion on their teeth caused by too much honey. Bath Abbey is breathtaking in its majesty and intricate detail. There is a warmth to the Abbey that invites me inside. I sit in the pew knowing I am staying too long but held captive by the stillness and beauty of the Abbey. The River of Life alter is mysteriously mesmerizing and the stone fan vaulting so overhead is breathtaking. This site has been a place of worship since the seventh century and there is a sense of authenticity in its being.

I haven't seen Carol or George or any of my fellow travelers in a while so I head to the place of meeting. By my calculations I am early so I wait patiently as others gather in the same location. There is a steady stream of rain so I snuggle into my hooded water proof jacket to wait on the tour bus. After a few minutes a bus arrives. I walk up intent on getting on board but I notice the guide is not Rita. The bus is from the same company with the same colors but it has a different number. The tour guide checks the schedule and shakes his head slowly. He informs me that my bus has already left. I stand there in stunned silence. How could this be? How could I miss an entire tour bus filled with people? How will I make it back to London? Rita's voice is echoing in my ears, "...and if you are not at this spot you will have to find your own way back to London for a minimum of £360." My stomach drops and my knees go weak. I do not have an extra $500 US dollars just for transportation. Ironically my jeans are now soaked by the pouring rain as I stand in the square, not quite sure what to do.

For several moments time stands still. The beauty of the architecture and the quaint shops fade. Bath is no longer warm or inviting, Salisbury and Stonehenge disappear from hopes. My cell phone does not work. I have no money to speak of and I am almost two hours from London. I am stranded and terrified. In my fog I inquire of strangers how to get back to London. Someone points vaguely toward a tourist information center. I wonder around the streets of Bath seeing nothing until I stumble upon the sign and walk into the center.

The center is warm and dry and well lit. I explain my predicament and the experienced guide replies with reassurance. There will be another bus along soon. All is not lost. I will not see Salisbury but the bus will stop at Stonehenge. I find my breath as hope returns to my rain soaked soul.

I am the first one on the bus to London via Stonehenge. When we stop at the amazing monument I am still tight with fear and apprehension. I record the appearance and clothing of several passengers and stay close to them as I explore to be sure the bus will not leave me.

As I approach the 5,000 year old site my heart begins to unclench. The sheer size of the stones dwarf the people and overwhelm the senses. The massive stones known as sarsens are up to 30 feet in height with their bases buried deep in the Salisbury plain. They weigh an average of 25 tons each. There are 83 stones in and around the circle. Some stones are sandstones, others have a blue tinge and are believed to have been transported over 140 miles from Wales. How the ancient travelers achieved this feat remains a part of the mystery. But the purpose of worship still lingers in the air.

I stand and stare absorbing the mystery and majesty of the scene. My soul is finally still enough to hear. My eyes are drawn to the top of the highest stone. There, on the very top overlooking the stone circle is a solitary bird. She is still, content; at home. The purpose of travel is to take you to new heights, she seems to stay. So never fear strange, new places, new circumstances or being alone. This is all a part of the journey and the majesty that is worship.

SuperMoon

The moon kissing the earth
in this dance of splendid ethereal love.
Now we skip the dance
And watch it on TV.

Two Rivers

The root of being is fed by two rivers
Fear and Love
Love grows slowly, offering new pathways into being
Fear is swift and fervent feeding on love like a parasite
until all that is left of the lovely oak
is the moss hanging from its dead branches.
Thus the work of being is the daily letting go of fears
and seeking contentment in the no-thing-ness of love.

The Beauty of Nothing

The brush touches the virgin canvas
The pen tastes the empty page
The mouth parts to utter a sound
The body inhales to flow with the out-breath
It's the moment of Nothing
Before there is everything.

124

Living on Pause

Pausing the breath to try really hard,
I can rest afterward.
Pausing belief for a bit of fear,
I mean, don't we all have worries and cares?
Pausing self-control for another slice of cake
I'll work it off, in the morning, once I awake!
Pausing faith to succumb to stress,
How else can I handle all duress?
Pausing my dreams to meet the needs of now
I'll make it, somehow
Pausing life for a little bit of death,
I can stop breathing, just for now.

Torreya Challenge
(Torreya State Park Trail)

Pines scrape the sky with spindly arms
While the waxy leaves of magnolias secret away
the moisture of yesterday's dew
The rain has carved bold accents in the land
giving valleys and bluffs
To replace the plains it has ravaged.
Above all is the wind, circling like an impatient mother
For it must birth change in its unending touch.

Bright green moss embellishes ubiquitous browns and grays
Bronze leaves float from empty branches
displaying the splendor of a graceful death.
The pink sands of the earth form the white stones
that line the riverbed
and mushroom thrive in random places.

125

Bring the Dawn

In the forest the lesson is concrete: growth is life.
Life and death thrive in each other's arms
unconcerned about what their merger may spawn
For their union in the moment is everything.

Powerful Peace

I invite Peace into the interstices of my being
into the darkened corners of my soul
into the blocked places in my brain
informing my thoughts
renewing my mind.

I invite Peace into my blood,
coursing through my veins like holy emissaries
lubricating my joints, empowering my movements.
filling my breath and the spaces
between my breath.

Peace, flow through me like a Spirit River
washing away fear and old,
stagnation and decay.
Open for me the rooms
long closed by doubt and delusion.

Flow Spirit River of Peace
Mighty rushing waters, flow!
Be my breath.
Be my blood.
Powerful Peace be My Being

Clyde's Call

Clyde's wife was an unfortunate woman, having married him at his peak. She hadn't known it then, thinking the peak but the foothills of his glory. By the time she realized she had been sentenced to co-labor in his miserable existence, it was too late. She was chained by a wedding band and he had fully ensconced himself in her life, burrowed beneath the surface of her soul like a well embedded tick.

"Pass me the remote will ya? And while ya at it, hand me a beer." Clyde used the weight of his ample belly to ease the La-Z-Boy way beyond the manufacturer's specifications. It creaked in protest but the sound was overshadowed by his own flatulence, the odor of which filled the room like a malevolent spirit.

Grace stepped around the small collection of beer cans that littered the small living room holding their 8 month old in one arm and herding the five and three year olds before her with her other hand. The older boys were dressed in their Sunday best. The tiny black pants and pastel shirts gave no indication that they had been obtained from Grace's diligent visits to the local thrift store. The little girl in her arms was an adorable bundle of pink lace and bows retrieved from her neighbor's Goodwill donation pile. Sue had not wanted to offend Grace by offering the clothes but asked her to drop the bag off for her. She had casually added, "If you see anything you like feel free to grab it before you drop it off." Grace herself was dressed in a sleek long sleeved black rayon dress with white collar and cuffs and a pair of black stilettos. The dress clung to her curvaceous figure denying the hardship of three births and two miscarriages. Clyde did not believe in birth control, or work for that matter. But he believed passionately in his right to eat, drink and procreate. He railed against the government but saw no contradiction in accepting the welfare check and medical services

127

it provided due to the strain of a one income household.

As she walked by her husband intent on ignoring his demands and getting the children to church, the older boy, CJ, broke away from his mother's guiding hand and ran to the refrigerator. He grabbed two beers and dashed past his mother, quickly handing one beer to his father while popping the top of the other. Before his mother could react he put the can to his lips, took a deep swig of the bitter liquid, grimaced then announced, "I don't want to go to Sunday School. I want to stay right here and have fun like Daddy." The three year old, Calen started after him but was restrained by his mother's tightening grip.

Clyde popped the beer open took a deep drink and guffawed. "A boy after mi own heart!" He declared, clapping CJ so hard on the back his beer spilled on to his freshly laundered blue shirt. That's when Grace decided she would kill her husband.

She had snatched up CJ and made him wash his mouth out with soap. They had left the untidy house and the slovenly man behind but Grace remembered none of that. When Pastor Clements exulted the virtues of patience and forgiveness she did not remember thinking him a fool. She did not remember going to the alter or the strange look the preacher gave her when she prayed aloud, "Lord if you don't do it, I will."

The next week transpired as they had for the last seven years of their marriage. Grace got up by 5 a.m. each day, prepared the children for school, dropped them off and went to her job as an office assistant in the probate division of a large state office building downtown. Before her marriage she had been taking advantage of the college tuition assistance and was enrolled in college courses at night. She had grown up in abject poverty, surrounded by four older sisters and a single mother. She was the only one of her sisters to graduate from high school with highest honors and she planned to be the first one to graduate from college.

She had earned her Associate in Arts degree and was only three
semesters away from her Bachelors of Arts in Criminology. This
was just the beginning for Grace. She had dreams of going to law
school and planned to become a defense attorney. Every night she
would practice offering her defense on behalf of some misguided
soul she had seen being arrested on the evening news. "Your
Honor, the defense intends to prove that this was a crime of
passion, brought about by the victim's own culpable negligence."
She didn't know what the legal terms meant yet but she enjoyed
arguing her point to her image in the mirror. She had no idea she
was preparing for her own defense.

She had met Clyde in the elevator on her way to one of her night
classes. He was handsome and svelte then. He had struck up a
conversation and seemed highly impressed with her energy,
ambition and beauty. Grace's office was on the 21st. floor and he
had entered the elevator on the ninth floor where the child welfare
office was located. He had brushed off her questions about why he
was in the building, implying that he was on a confidential child
enforcement case involving a dead beat dad. She had no idea until
after the birth of their first child that he had been the offender in
the case he pretended to investigate. Clyde had sired seven other
children before he met Grace, none of which he supported. He had
just moved from one woman to the next, using the resources of the
current woman to support the demands of the previous family he
had created until he was thrown out or forced to find a new host.

In Grace Clyde had recognized the motherlode of potential
therefore he played his cards with stealth and cunning. He had
come to the state office building to attempt to defer judgments
against himself but he saw the opportunity of a lifetime in Grace.
So while he claimed a disability to delay judgements against him,
he had applied for disability benefits. The slow grind of the welfare
system delayed any proof of his fraud while he worked to capture
Grace's heart, and soul. There were flowers and chocolates of
course, followed by impromptu cards and invitations to lunch. He

made sure that each time she saw him he was well dressed and manicured, the very picture of success in his borrowed black Lexus. He studied her likes and dislikes, her passions and her weaknesses. He used Camille's credit card to lavish on Grace the dream of a perfect romance. By the time the credit card's limit had been reached, and Camille discovered the monthly bills demanding payment in the backyard trash, Clyde had already charged the cost of the tuxedo for his wedding to Grace.

Their wedding had been a simple affair. Grace, a lover of simplicity and balance had not wanted a big expensive church wedding. She had chosen instead an intimate setting with minister Pastor Clements, her mother, sisters and her best friends. Clyde had scraped up a handful of friends who spent most of their time gawking at the bride and drinking up the champagne. Grace did not complain when he took her to the local Days Inn Motel for their honeymoon. It was clean and comfortable and she believed him when he said he was saving money to buy their first home. She had laughed at the fact that her new husband had only his tuxedo and the clothes he had changed into after the wedding. She had no way of knowing that when Camille discovered the duplicity of her lover she had burnt all of his possessions in a giant bonfire in the backyard. When the fire department had arrived she had simply explained that their warning on code violation was better than a charge of homicide. She would have killed Clyde in her anger but he had escaped with only the clothes on his back and the tuxedo in his hand.

But that had been seven years ago. Grace had borne one indignity after another as she slowly discovered the true nature of her husband. Her dreams of finishing college and going to law school lay in a pile of ashes in her heart. She had never been a weak woman but she had been an innocent, unfamiliar with duplicity, when Clyde entered her life. He had skillfully manipulated her through subtle emotional abuse until she was no longer sure of her way. But on the Sunday morning that her five year old son drank his first taste of beer in an attempt to imitate his father something inside her snapped. It wasn't a crack but a snap. Something snapped into place. She suddenly saw the last seven years as if viewing it all from a place of dispassionate understanding. She saw the cycle of poverty and deception from her parents to her now taking root in her child. She saw her son become his father, using and abusing his way through countless women and leaving a sea of hopeless, fatherless children in his wake. She saw it all and knew it must end, knew she must end it if her children were to have any hope at all.

One rainy morning two weeks later she awoke as usual to ready herself and the children for school. She dressed in the darkness of pre-dawn's last embrace, then bent over her husband's sleeping hulk and whispered,
"It is time for you to get up and help with the children." It was a simple request really, one that she had made with many passionate pleas in the early years of their marriage. But her requests had been drowned out, while she had been shoved around and berated as an ineffective mother. But this morning her voice was different, soft and almost tender. Clyde would have ignored her voice in his ear if it had not been for a certain unnerving calm in it he had never heard before. That and a clicking sound piqued his curiosity. His eyes focused in the dark to see his wife holding his favorite cigarette lighter. His mind grappled with the meaning of the flame until a sudden heat in the lower portion of his pyjamas arrested his attention. Clyde squawked and bolted out of bed trying to put out the small flames that enveloped the ends of his pants. His attempts seemed to fan the flames and in his panic he bolted out of the room, through the front door and into the pouring rain. Still screaming he threw himself on to the ground and rolled around until the flames were fully extinguished.

He had collected himself when he reentered the house and was determined to unload the full power of his wrath on his wife. But when he entered the front door she was standing there, waiting, in the fullness of her new found calm, holding the lighter in one hand and his cell phone in the other. "If you touch me I will burn everything you own." Her words weren't threatening. They were a simple statement of fact. Somewhere in his memory the picture of a homicidal Camille burning everything he owned resurfaced like an omen.

By this time the children had been awakened by the commotion and were clamoring for attention. Clyde did not help that morning. He had never bothered to learn what to do so he couldn't have helped if he wanted to. But he hung around the fringes of the activity like an animal whose nest had been disturbed.

The next morning when the same calm voice summoned him to get up and help with his children he roused himself quickly checking his pants and his surroundings for signs of fire. No fire, no lighter. He didn't realize he had been holding his breath until he heard himself sigh. He would have convinced himself that the fire in his bed had been a nightmare if it had not been for the pair of pajamas sitting on his night stand. It was the pair he had been wearing the previous morning. They had been laundered and were neatly folded. He reached for them with unsteady hands. He shook the pants loose only to find that they had been neatly cut to just below the knees. It was at that moment that his legs began to sting. It all came rushing back. Last night Grace had come home from work and dropped a tube of aloe vera ointment into his lap saying, "You should have just got up and helped." His legs were slightly burned and it had occurred to him that had he been in his right mind he would have just stripped off the burning pants right away and beat some sense into the woman. But this was a new Grace. He wasn't quite sure how to handle this one. In the past when a woman started acting crazy he would just leave her for the one he had groomed to take her place. But he had let himself get complacent with Grace. She made decent money and was timid. All it had taken to keep her in line were a few slaps here and there and some insults. With life this easy he hadn't bothered to groom her replacement. He had no place to go.

He left the bedroom for the only place that made sense, the kitchen table. But Grace did not stop what she was doing to make his eggs. In fact when she finally came in the kitchen she had baby Hope in her hands. "She needs to be changed." With that she plopped the baby on his lap and walked away. Poor Hope would have slid to the floor if she had not grabbed a fist full of her father's chest hairs. "Aaagh!" Clyde opened his mouth to scream and caught a whiff of Hope's diaper. He tried to put the baby down but her little fits were clasped tightly around his hairs.
"Grace!" He expected his wife to dutifully appear and take the smelly baby but out of the corner of his eyes he saw Grace appear with his cell phone and the lighter.
"Damn!" he mumbled under his breath. "This has got to stop!" He held the baby close and took her into the room for a changing. His mind rebelled and his anger swelled. "No woman going to handle me like that," he mumbled under his breath. He decided right then and there that he was going to handle this through the only way he knew: Violence.

Grace had plans of her own. She knew that by now her husband would no longer be willing to put up with her gentle attempts of re-direction. It was time to follow through on her decision.

That evening Grace and the children didn't come home. Clyde paced around the small living room like an enraged bull. He called her cell phone and left messages until it was full. He called her mother, her job, her sisters, her friends. No one answered. To make matters worse the woman hadn't left any cooked food in the house and the beers were all gone. He used the debit card to order some pizza.
"Declined? What you mean declined? Run it again!" He tried three different pizza places. The answer was always the same. He finally poured himself some of the children's cereal with milk and ate three soup bowls full. He switched on the television to wait until

his wife got home. He was going to make her regret her little pranks. That much he knew.

"What the hell is wrong with the television?" It took him several minutes before he realized the cable had been switch off. By now Clyde was so angry he couldn't sit still. He paced back and forth banging his fist into the door and yelling. He should have saved his energy.

Twenty one nights later Clyde awakened with a start. He had been surviving by cooking random supplies in the cupboard and on the kindness of friends. He had even worked a few days as the clean-up guy at the local mechanic's shop to get himself some necessities. Each night he came home and found himself alone in a house that now felt like a tomb. He would lie in bed for hours trying to figure out how to deal with this sudden and drastic change in his life. Never before had he found himself without the help he had always taken for granted. He missed the chaos of his children running around the house bumping into the furniture. He missed a home cooked meal. He missed the quiet strength of his wife. He laid in his bed starting into the blackness of the night, sleep as elusive as a future. The house was deathly still. It was so quite he could hear himself breathe. He had tried to find Grace and the children for three weeks. He had gone by her mother's house but Grace wasn't there and her mother refused to talk to him threatening to call the police. Her friends and sisters had done the same. He had been to her job but they said Grace was on vacation. None of it made any sense to him. Who goes on vacation for three weeks with no money? His thoughts followed the same endless loop they had for the past three weeks.

 "Lord forgive me for what I'm about to do." Clyde froze when he heard that same soft almost tender voice like a ghost whispering in his ear. He started to sit up but something cold and hard was at his throat. He froze.

"I wouldn't worry about the knife," Grace whispered softly. It's the hypodermic needle that should concern you. That's when Clyde felt the slight pin prick pressure on the right side of his neck. He broke into a cold sweat.

"Grace, you gone crazy?!" He didn't mean for his voice to squeak like that. He was a man, not some weak ass punk! "You leave a mark on me and you going to jail!" He yelled with venomous conviction.

"Nooo. I don't think so Clyde," Grace said calmly.

"You see, everybody has seen you hunting me down and threatening me over the past three weeks. Plus this needle is filled with liquid crack complements of your buddy Dingo. You even flinch and this needle will deliver your death."

"What the ..." Clyde was too overcome with shock to utter the expletive.

"I've been thinking about this for some time now Clyde." Grace sounded calm and patient as if she was talking to their three year old Calen.

"Everything you have, I bought. You took my money, my dreams and my self-respect. So if you're foolish enough to move tonight I get all of that back."

"You'll never get away with this Grace." his voice was cracking again. It was dark but he could tell she wasn't bluffing. He could beat her but if he moved to grab her that needle could accidently pierce his jugular. He felt the cold boney specter of death enter the room, anticipating a victory.

As if reading his mind Grace continued, "If you do escape the needle and the knife I have a gun complements of your friend Dingo."

"You're lying!" This was just getting ludicrous he thought. "Dingo is my homeboy. He wouldn't do this to me!"

"Dingo may be a drug dealer Clyde but he has a mother; a mother whose husband beat her and left her to care for him and his five brother and sisters. How many of your kids do you care for Clyde?"

He swallowed carefully afraid the movement might disturb the knife or the needle.

"If I have to cut your throat I have my defense. I practiced it for years Clyde. It was meant to be used in a court of law for some other poor soul. You wanna hear it Clyde?"

What could he say? His mind was racing down a barren road with no end in sight.

"Your Honor, she continued," the defense intends to prove that this was a crime of passion, brought about by the victim's own culpable negligence." Grace's words cooled the blood in Clyde's veins. It was as if she had already killed him but he was right there listening to the defense of the act. In his desperation his mind veered off its track and he found himself in a wide open field of new thought.

"Grace?" His voice was raspy with fear and anticipation.

"Grace, ww-what if I changed?"

"A leopard never changes his spots!" She spat this with so much venom he flinched.

"But I have reason to change Grace. I wanna live.... and, and we have the kids Grace! They need a father!"

"Ha! You a father?" But Clyde pressed him point sensing an opportunity.

"Wait Grace! I'll get a job! You won't have to pay my child support payments anymore. I'll work and help take care of the kids....I'll even go to church.... and you can go back to school Grace!"

"Grace, you are a Christian woman. God doesn't want you to do this!"

"I'll change Grace! God knows I will!" Clyde's conversion though inspired by an unholy terror, was fervent and sincere.

Grace was almost drunk with the violence of her intent but Clyde's words beckoned to her. They spoke of all the hope she had lost. With the needle still gently scraping the side of his neck, Grace removed the knife from his throat and stuck it in the waistband of her skirt. She used her free hand to turn on the lamp next to her then reached into the drawer of the night stand and pulled out a legal writing pad with a pen clipped to it.

"So you think you can change? I want that in blood or in ink. The choice is yours," She dropped the pen and pad on the mound that was his stomach then brought the knife back to his throat. And so the negotiation for his life began.

Another seven years later Clyde sat in the large auditorium with Pastor Clements, on either side of him sitting quietly were his sons CJ and Calen. They were neatly dressed in clean white shirts and khaki pants, their hands folded patiently holding noisemakers in their laps. His daughter Hope sat on his lap wearing her fancy Easter dress and matching blue ribbons. The graduation march sounded and Grace's name was called. The boys jumped up smashing the noisemakers against their lips as they blew loud and tuneless noises into the air. Clyde stood too holding on to a squirming Hope who craned her neck to catch a glimpse of her mother. He watched his wife walk across the stage and beam a smile at her family as she extended her hand to receive her Doctor of Jurisprudence diploma. Beside them sat Pastor Clements shaking his head in amazement.

"Clyde I am so proud of Grace but I am equally proud of you! If you hadn't heard the call and come on into the church none of this would have been possible."

Clyde's gathered his children as they prepared to head out and celebrate with the new graduate. His mind flashed back to the night that had changed his life. It was a call all right. He shook his head to clear it of the vivid memories. Then he smiled and nodded quietly.

"You sure right about that Pastor. You sure right."

Paralysis of Fear

How do you dry out a soul wet with apathy?
How do you feed someone not hungry
for life, for transformation, for a dream?

How do you free a mind encased in inertia?
It is the job of Spirit, not human hands.
Intercession and patience are all we can command.

WON'T

Won't do;
Won't get up;
Won't straighten up.

Won't yield
to any hope trying to enter.
Won't try
anything that will make the situation better.
Won't consider another way
Won't make good use of the day
Or any other treasure God or Man throws their way.

When someone won't
It's like trying to light wet wood.
In a forest fully ablaze this kindling won't catch
This fire won't burn.
Foxes, deer and rabbits are running for their lives
but this dog won't hunt.
It lies in the midst of action
Paralyzed by fear.

Slow Death

Did Rome fall with a blazing crash?
Or was that just the outward sign?
Did joy leave in a huff?
Or were there many little discontents?
Did I suddenly grow old?
Or did I harden a little at a time?
Will I just one day die?
Or will I suffer a thousand little deaths along the way?

Bring the Dawn

Intercession

Keeper of the Keys to every heart
Unlock the doors that fear has bolted shut
Light the wick wet with tears and fears and apathy
Illumine the path to freedom for those bound in Oblivion.

Lead, by Your Spirit, Lord
Those imprisoned in heart and mind
by a master whose name is Death.
Awaken Your living Army
A community of intercessors.

Instruct us as You did in days of old
To circle the walls in faithfulness and praise.
For the deliverance that will come
When we shout in Your Name.

Listen

Drowning in a sea of inertia
God is not a man that He should lie
Gasping for air in a fetid world
Wait I say on The Lord
Starving for freedom from the status quo
Be of good courage
I can't hold on, I'm drowning
Wait, I say on The Lord.

139

A Beautiful Thing

Believing is a head thing, a mind thing, even an ego thing
Knowing is a deep thing, a heart thing, even a cellular thing
And when knowing surfaces from the deep
it changes head and heart and mind
and displays as a beautiful thing.

Megabus Ride

Modernity has separated us from our roots
and sometimes that is good.
The Babylonians, the Mesopotamians
the Egyptians, Romans and the Greeks
all had a hand in inventing soap
But it was sparing and discrete.

As I stand within the waiting throng,
the traveling coach close at hand
I gasp wondering what has gone wrong.
I am reminded that in ancient times
the great unwashed was the common man
and this strong smell ran throughout the land.

Technology has taken us to new found heights
and that's as it should.
Those two Frenchmen brought this same soap
to the likes of you and me
But some of us refuse to be set free.
This strange smell, the under arms unwashed
that meets my nose unabashed
would be the norm of the day, a century ago
But today, it has to go.

No one has told my seat mate

Bring the Dawn

That soap would improve his life
beside him I must ride
for four long hours into the night
My sense of smell losing the fight.

He sits so close in this luxury coach
out of his pocket falls a roach
His hair unkempt his clothes unwashed
He, an enemy of the toothbrush
He reeks of old and stale, and ancient ways
Things we wash with soap these days.

I thank the Babylonians, the Mesopotamians
the Egyptians, Romans and the Greeks
and finally those Frenchmen who made soap so cheap
With this guy beside me I'm gonna need a heap!

The Lollipop Man

He was a civil servant once you see
He lives to serve, to meet a need.
Help the children cross the street
Be kind to everyone you meet.
He's the Lollipop Man
And his beat's the street.

He cannot afford to take a wife
Money is tight in his lonely life.
He can't see your face
But he'll help you still
His purpose is helping,
It is his skill.

Need some help to cross the street?
He's the one you want to meet.

141

Bring the Dawn

Needing a bus or help to stand?
No need to worry
He'll lend you a hand.
He's the Lollipop Man
And his beat's the street.

He will give you his spare change.
His whole day he'll re-arrange
His purpose is helping
It is his skill.
He's the Lollipop Man
And his beat's the street.

<u>Air-Travel</u>

I have a friend who is afraid to fly.
He has many reasons why.
The best one is, he may die.
I shake my head and sigh.
How can I say it's worth the pain
When he sees me whine and complain?

ORLANDO

Jeannie snatched the barbequed chicken leg out of Sam's hand while he was in mid-bite, leaving his mouth gaping open and empty except for the smearing of sauce at the corners.
"You have GOT to come with me to London!" The urgency in her voice bordered on desperation.
Sam's deprived lips quivered before his teeth clamped shut in resignation to his disappointment. He glared at Jeannie who had moved out of arms reach with his food. She glared back with that steely glint she always got when she dug her heels in on an issue. She is a stubborn one for sure, Sam mused as he swallowed his unfulfilled saliva. In the thirty years he had known this woman he could not ever remember winning an argument. She had talked him into more cockamamie schemes and more trouble than most convicted felons had committed, he was sure.

It was true, her 5' 2 frame and unremarkable appearance belied the volume of mischief she was able to manufacture. She was a small woman with walnut brown skin, cinnamon colored eyes and fawn colored hair. But from the day they met in an integrated first grade classroom some 30 years ago Jeannie had introduced an element of risk into his life. Age had not dulled her attraction to danger. Sam knew this was the element that had kept their friendship fresh all these years. He was careful to the point of obsession and Jeannie flew by the seat of her pants. She was the yang to his yin.

But this time he had to stand his ground. He was not going to fly.

143

Ever. She could not even fully articulate the reason for this sudden need to fly almost four thousand miles across the world. She had babbled on about a pregnant aunt and a looming family crisis. But his friend was going to have to take her chances in a foreign land on her own. He would stay right here in sunny Florida while she risked life and limb for some suddenly apparent sense of filial piety.

He lifted his ample frame from his loveseat, and with a speed that belied his size, reached over and snatched back the chicken leg from her hand. Before she could react he opened his mouth and stuffed the entire drumstick in. He gnawed on the leg long enough to pull off all the meat. Dropping the bare bone onto the plate she was still holding, Sam chewed slowly and deliberately for several seconds. When he had reduced his wad of meat to a manageable size he opened his mouth, showing shreds of partially chewed meat mingled with sauce and uttered one sound, "No!!"

Finding himself at the airport check-in counter, Sam was still not sure how he came in possession of a ticket to London. Not only did he have no interest in flying, he became nauseatingly ill on roller coasters and was terrified of heights. So why was he telling the attendant that he would be checking one suitcase and had one carry-on? No sooner was he in possession of his boarding pass than it was snatched out of his hand. Jeannie, the consummate control freak had grabbed the boarding pass and was rushing him out of line. "We board at gate B. Hurry, it's a long way!" She grabbed his carry-on to hurry him along.
"Hey! My medicines are in that!" He was not a fan of exercise or any other fast movement. In fact he was not a fan of movement at all, but Sam found himself trotting beside his lifelong friend as she headed for the gate.
When they arrived at the departure gate Sam was dripping with sweat and out of breath. "I can't do this Jeannie, I'm too scared.."
"It will be okay Sam, we have your medicine right here." She patted his carry-on. In it was an opened bottle of Dramamine

which Jeannie had borrowed from her mother's medicine cabinet. She wouldn't let him have one. They were not even in the air yet. She was waiting for just the right time to play this ace.

By the time they boarded the airplane Sam's whining had reached its zenith.
"Jeannie, I thought you said this was going to be fun! Orlando to London is actually -
Orlando airport:
- pour out my water
- take off my shoes
- take off my belt
- get a quick dose of a radioactive scan
- get patted down
- buy airport water for five times the price
- get forced at the last minute to check my carry-on
- board the airplane
- wait, wait, wait
- now I'm without my stuff, only to find there is lots of room for my little bag in the overhead compartment of the plane. I hope I get my carry-on back in London!" Without seeming to breathe, he continued, "Meanwhile we will be stuck waiting for hours in Philadelphia, without all the snacks we packed." Finally he paused in his litany of complaints to dislodge his seat belt from under his rotund rear.
"At least we were able to grab your bag of meds before you had to check your carry-on," Jeannie was thinking if Sam didn't shut up soon it would be time to give him one of those Dramamines.

"But all our food is still in the carry-on and there's no meal on this flight!" Sam whined. "These seats are ridiculously small!" he continued, "And that woman had the nerve to say I should have purchased two seats! Who says that?!" he demanded. He snatched his elbow in and stuffed his legs under the seat in front of him just before the flight attendant reached above him to close the overhead bin. He was seated in the aisle seat beside Jeannie and the flight attendant assigned to that section of the airplane continually bumped into his elbow or knee as she walked the cabin.

Sam was used to insults. His characteristic Downs Syndrome features had made him the brunt of all manner of cruel jokes growing up. But he had been a fast learner who had given as good as he got. His jovial personality and quick wit had done more to win people over than the lectures about the rights of people with disabilities his teachers offered his classes. Now that people were more informed on disabilities he rarely suffered direct insults due to his draw from the communal gene pool. However his somewhat rotund figure was not a protected class under the ADA so Sam sometimes had to deal with the sting of being judged by his weight.

When the airplane began its taxi down the runway with increasing speed Sam grasped the armrests with white knuckles. His face turned an ashen shade of blue. "Breathe Sam!" Jeannie whispered to him and took the hand closest to her in a gesture of comfort. The airplane lifted off and so did Sam. His behind literally left the seat and his body strained against the lap belt. Jeannie looked on with alarm, afraid he too would be airborne within the cabin. He remained rigid and strained against his seatbelt, tense and unmoving for several minutes as the airplane ascended. "Breathe!" she whispered urgently, squeezing his hand and rubbing his shoulder. Finally the airplane leveled off and Sam's body plopped back into his seat as he let out a bellowing breath. That's when Jeannie realized that she too had been holding her breath in sympathy of her friend's distress. The journey was just beginning, she had to distract him or he would never get on the connecting flight!

Having dragged her friend out of his comfort zone, Jeannie was anxious for his experience to be a good one. She watched the activity in the cabin like a new mother monitoring the safety and comfort of her newborn. He struggled to get comfortable in a seat so small it should have qualified as a fire safety hazard. She was sure that he would be hard pressed to leave the extreme confines of his seat in time to make it to the lavatory much less escape in the event of an emergency.

Sam was not alone in feeling the restriction of space. One of a pair of twin toddlers sat comfortably behind Jeannie. His identical twin and his mother, with earphones plugged in her ears, were seated across the aisle from him. The mother was a small frazzled looking woman who tapped on the screen of her cell phone. She managed her electronic game with intense interest while her boys wiggled, squirmed and whined. But the man seated behind Sam was about 6'4" and was confined to approximately 12 inches of leg room. His every breath seemed to cause his body to expand, resulting in his knobby knees poking into Sam's back like a maniacal massage for much of the journey. Gratefully, exhaustion overtook him and he folded like an unwilling pretzel for a brief nap. Surely true rest is not possible on these inflexible birds, Sam mused as he watched the joyless flight attendants police the aisles with intermittent offerings of a service devoid of hospitality. Since the airline had taken to inflight advertising of certain products, Sam found himself being offered credit cards and other products. He watched with fascination as the hapless flight attendants, forced to peddle the latest sales item, walked up and down the aisle calling out in almost apologetic voices as they interrupted their captives' already fitful sleep.

Unlike his 6' 4" masseur behind him, Sam could not find the doorway into rest. He determined that sleeping on an airplane required the gift of the contortionist. He leaned over and grumbled to Jeannie that the seats were designed for sleeping as much as the electric chair was designed for relaxation. "You may as well be laid out on an ancient torture rack," he complained.

"Sam, let's have a drink." The flight attendant was heading toward them with a cart.
"Jeannie, you know I don't drink," Sam chided. But Jeannie

pressed the issue.

"This is a celebration. It's your first flight. We are headed to London for the first time. And plus, it will help you relax a bit." She added the last line a bit more timidly. The cart was two seats away. "Come on Sam, just a glass of wine, my treat." That was how she had talked him into trying kimchee, couscous, tofu and a host of other foods he would never have touched if he'd been left to his own devices. He had to admit to himself that over all the experiences were good, so why not?

"Okay," he muttered. Three glasses of wine later, Sam was a mellow fellow. Jeannie had to cut him off when he reached for the flight attendant call button to order another glass. "Now who is uptight?" Sam grumbled, his words slurring slightly as he settled into his little seat with new found flexibility. Before Jeannie could answer him, he let out a snort followed by a cacophony of snoring that shook the cabin.

Feeling her charge safe in the arms of sleep she gratefully relaxed, then dozed off. She was awakened in the darkness of the cabin by a strong rocking. Her sleep addled consciousness could not figure out what was happening. Her mind grasped the tendrils of fear. Turbulence? Engine malfunction? Terrorist attack?

"Oh God!" But it was none of these. Sam was snoring quietly beside her. She looked around the cabin for clues. All was peaceful. The movement was coming from directly behind her seat. She peered around to discover that the second boy had joined his twin in the seat behind her while their mother lay with her head against the window, either unconcerned or unaware of what was going on around her. The boys were in the heights of a wrestling frenzy with her seat back as a buffer zone. Jeannie sat seething while the boys kicked and yanked the back of her seat, oblivious of her ire. Maybe I should take a Dramamine, she thought wryly. The WWF match only ended when the flight attendant insisted everyone return to their seats in preparation for landing. She had to buckle the young wrestlers in since their mother never emerged from her blanket until the airplane bumped unto the tarmac.

148

PHILADELPHIA

In Philadelphia they deplaned for their long layover. The wine and the nap had relaxed Sam enough for him to endure the landing. But Jeannie was sure she saw claw marks on his armrest where he had clutched it during the descent unto the runway. The normally gregarious Sam was strangely silent as they sat at the gate. Jeannie practically dragged him to the food area to find a meal. Unfortunately, the first food vendor boasted an $11 price tag for a bagel and a cup of coffee. Sam was nothing if not frugal. He dropped the bagel back on the shelf as if it had burned him and walked away. Her normally curious friend was not interested in checking out other food area. She tried convincing him to walk around and window shop but he refused that as well.

Shortly before boarding Sam headed to the men's room. Jeannie pulled out a copy of the inflight magazine and thumbed through it as she waited. Slowly a sense of unease began to grow in her stomach. The airline personnel had walked over to the desk and were preparing to begin the boarding call. Where was Sam? She grabbed her bags and headed toward the restrooms.
"Sam?" Jeannie stood outside the Men's room and tentatively poked her head in the doorway.
"Sam!" Her unease was turning into distress. "Excuse me Sir. Did you see another man in there? He's wearing a blue jacket and jeans." The man exiting the rest room shook his head without even looking at her and kept going.
"Now boarding Flight 7345 to London, Heathrow." The airport intercom announced.
"Sam!!" This time there was a tinge of panic in Jeannie's voice. Looking quickly around to see if any other men were on the way in to the rest room she ventured tentatively into the Men's room.
"What the...?!" an older man glared at her with shock and reproach as he exited a stall.
"Sorry, I'm looking for my friend. It's almost time to leave and..."

He did not stay to wash his hands or to listen to her explanation but brushed by her making a quick exit.

"Sam!!" Jeannie squatted down and looked for feet in the only locked stall. Her heart leapt as she spotted Sam's tennis shoes.

"Sam!! It's time to go!" she yelled urgently.

"I'm not getting on that plane!" Sam's empathic voice boomed from behind the door.

"What?! Sam this is no time for that. We have to go!"

I'm NOT going. You go on by yourself. I am not flying anywhere!" His voice held an edge Jeannie had not heard before. "Sam are you out of your mind?? We are in Philadelphia! They are boarding our flight! Our tickets are paid for and even if you don't go to London, you would have to fly back home!" Her mind was racing for the arguments that would convince Sam to come out of the stall.

Nothing worked. Her unease grew into full blown panic. She didn't even notice the men giving her unwelcome glances as they walked into the restroom. As her mind raced her body acted. She got down on all fours and began a rapid army crawl under the door of Sam's stall. She grimaced as her body came in contact with the restroom floor. She willed her mind not to think about it as she squeezed her small frame through the limited space. He was sitting on the toilet with his pants up but the intrusion sent him scrambling and he yelled at her with the dilated pupils of a cornered animal.

"Get out Jeannie! I mean it. I'm not flying! You can't talk me into this one." I tried it and I don't like it. I don't want to die!"

"What's going on in there?" a male voice said from the other side of the door. "I'm going to call security." The voice was replaced by the sound of steps walking out of the room.

Jeannie grabbed him and they began to struggle in the close space. "You are afraid of dying? Well what you think TSA is going to do to you when they find you in here hiding? Huh?"

Sam paused in his struggles and Jeannie pressed her advantage. "Terrorist! That's what they're gonna think Sam! You think the little security scan was invasive? Wait till they put you in that little room and do a full body cavity search! You afraid of being in the air? Well how about jail? Those cells are small too and that's

where they're gonna send you!"
Sam's eyes sobered as the weight of her words began to sink in.
"But I didn't do anything. They have no reason to hold me." His
resolve was weakening. Jeannie pressed her advantage. She spoke
quickly and urgently.
"Yeah, sure. But they don't know that. They are trained to think
you are guilty until proven otherwise. How do you prove you
DIDN'T do something? Like planting a bomb in this bathroom
stall?"
Sam's eyes narrowed, "What?! I see what you're doing Jeannie!
You are trying to manipulate me!"
"Of course I am! I want you to get on that flight! I may be way off
base but TSA is on their way so it's fly or face them, Sam!" She
stared at him intently. Their breath mingled in the small space. For
one interminable moment nothing moved. Then Sam blinked and
his pupils narrowed. He took a deep breath. "Okay, I'll go with
you." Jeannie's body sagged with relief but she didn't notice her
own reaction. She pulled the latch on the stall's door, grabbed her
bags and rushed to the sink to wash her hands and face . "Quick,
turn your jacket inside out and put on your baseball cap!"
"What?! Why?"
The intercom interrupted them, "Finally boarding call for Flight
7345 to London Heathrow."
"In case someone saw you coming in, it will be harder for them to
identify you." Jeannie was busy putting on the pink sweater from
her carry-on bag.
Finally feeling the same sense of urgency, Sam quickly complied.
"Let's go!" she grabbed his hand and they walked quickly out of
the restroom. They rounded the corner and headed to the gate as
two TSA agents came running toward the Men's room.

Sam kept up with Jeannie as they dashed to the gate and gave the
agent their boarding passes. They ran down the corridor to the
airplane and made it inside the cabin door as the flight personnel
were reaching to close the door.

The cabin of the Airbus was significantly more spacious than on their previous flight. As they approached their assigned seats the female passenger already seated in their row was busy arguing with an older couple standing next to the seats in front of her. The couple was carrying a case which housed a small Yorkshire terrier. The flight attendant had to intervene to assure the woman that indeed, the small dog was allowed on international flights per the airlines' policies. Having lost that argument the woman looked up from her seat and glared at them even as they approached their places. Even at a glance Jeannie could tell that life, like an un-ripened fruit picked prematurely had given this woman only bitter and sparing joy. The blight was reflected in her shriveled and unyielding countenance. She obviously resented having to let them through to their seats. They had to squeeze by her spindly legs and stiffly turned body.

Much to Jeannie's relief Sam's seat was larger than his seat on the previous flight and was next to the window this time. She reasoned to herself that having Sam in the window seat would allow a buffer, bringing less attention to them, should Sam have another meltdown. She was seated in the middle seat beside him. Meanwhile the passenger beside her sat rigid and unapproachable.

Once they were seated and belted in Jeannie set to work trying to distract Sam from any looming distress. She knew he was a fan of numbers and statistics so she offered him a bone to chew on, "Sam, this is pretty amazing stuff!" She pointed to the monitor which displayed information about their flight.

"We are traveling over 3,653 miles in six hours entirely suspended over the vastness of the Atlantic Ocean. We are moving at an airspeed of 535 miles per hour that's an average ground speed of 580 mph. We are at an altitude of 39,000 feet above sea level and the temperature outside the airplane is -79 degrees Fahrenheit. Just trying to wrap my mind around it leaves me feeling small."

Notwithstanding all his doubts, Sam had to admit that the marvel of being airborne in a large metal bird was unmistakable. He relaxed his stiff frame and ventured a glance out the window as she spoke. Visually, the beautiful cloud-scape displayed the inescapable beauty of the land of the angels. The physical evidence of a greater whole opened his heart to majesty and soothed his mind. I can do this, he thought.

Nowhere was the stinginess of the airline more apparent than in their meals. During the flight the little 5"x 2" plastic container of bland rice grains and two pale, limp asparagus stalks with an artichoke leaf and a sad wedge of lemon comprised Jeannie's vegan dinner. Sam at least had a handful of lasagna. He looked over at her meal with pity. The container was just deep enough to hold a small mouse, who would probably have been more tasty, judging from the look on Jeannie's face. The rock hard white flour bagel, the size of a baby's fist, promised no nutrition or flavor but suggested possible constipation. One taste of her dinner and not even Jeannie's hunger could convince her to proceed. She returned it, including the unopened bagel and Sam wondered if she had lost some sadistic bid for the most unappealing meal.
Most of this misery presumably could have been avoided for a significant upgrade. They watched the flight attendants take seemingly tasty treats behind the curtain up front to people reclined in spacious seats, but since neither of them were willing to offer another month's salary for a few hours of comfort they endured the restrictions of economy class.

Sam's discomfort did not go entirely unnoticed. There was the occasional angel of the sky among the stiff-lipped stewards; the flight attendant who seemed to be there to ease their pains and calm their fears. She cruised up and down the aisle arriving with that extra blanket after they had been told they are out. She handed them extra cream for their coffee and smiled at them each time she walked by. She seemed to sense Sam's apprehension offering him earphones, extra drinks and slipping him extra snacks.

The nuances of air travel are reduced to their rightful size when

153

strangers share and together they poke fun at their surroundings and themselves. Sam was introduced to that stranger through the rambunctious antics of a little black Yorkie in the seat in front of him. The little dog belonged to an elderly British couple returning home from their holiday in Florida. The little Yorkie, determined to be free, escaped the confines of his carrying case and jumped onto the lap of the grim passenger beside Jeannie. She reacted violently, convulsing and pushing the little dog away from her. Assured of her adorability, the Yorkie trotted over to Jeannie's lap accepting her caresses before making her way to Sam's lap. Sam had to laugh, despite himself. He was terribly fond of dogs and the little black Yorkie with splashes of brown, perky ears and shiny jet black eyes and nose captured his heart instantly. Soon Sam was chattering away with the couple. Jeannie smiled to herself as she watched them get swept up in deep conversation despite their obvious differences. Sam at least for the moment seemed to have suspended his fears in favor of social interaction. Their aerial experiences validated, they settled into comfortable silence as they were rushed through space and time.

Soon the bustle subsided, the cabin lights dimmed and it was time for the long haul over the Atlantic. If it was at all possible, this should have been a time to rest.

In the dimmed cabin, Sam was still. Jeannie relaxed her vigilance and drifted into a light doze. Sam stared wide eyed into the darkness wondering how to rein in his galloping mind. The what-ifs crept out from behind the tiny thread of faith he had in his safety. Soon he was sweating and his breathing was turning shallow. He adjusted his air control and removed his jacket but it didn't help. The cabin was closing in on him. He had to get some space. He pushed up the window shade. But the black expanse outside his window brought him no comfort. Still he had to look. There must be something out there that would give him hope that the metal bird was not plummeting to his death. Suddenly he was shaking Jeannie with a rough hand.

"What?!" she was shocked into alertness and alarm simultaneously.

"Look!" Sam said gesturing out the window.

"What?"

"There! On the wing!"

"What?!" Jeannie stretched her body across him for a better view but saw nothing.

"Don't you see them?!" Sam's voice was rising. This was not good.

"See what?" Jeannie whispered, hoping he'd take the cue and lower his voice.

"There! On the wing! There are two of them!" His voice was only getting louder.

"Two of what Sam?" Jeannie whispered even more quietly.

"Not what. Who! There are two of them!!" Now he was gesturing wildly toward the wing. This was definitely not good.

"Sam, keep your voice down. People are trying to sleep." Jeannie whispered sharply.

But Sam's eyes were wide, his pupils fully dilated in the dimness of the cabin light.

"But they are right there! Flying alongside the airplane! Two of them. Don't you see them??"

Passengers nearby were starting to stir. Jeannie thought quickly, if she lied and said yes, it might put an end to the scene that was brewing. Before she could solve her moral dilemma a harsh voice cut loudly through her thoughts.

"People are trying to sleep. Be quiet!" It was the voice of woman beside her. She glowered at them in the darkness. But by now Sam was tapping on the insulated glass of his window and making beaconing gestures. He was oblivious to the scene he was creating in the cabin.

The woman snapped at them again, awakening the sleeping baby across the aisle. He began to wail in earnest. The little Yorkie in front wiggled free from her sleeping owner and bounded over the top of the seat unto the prudish passenger's lap. She yelled even louder. The Yorkie trotted across Jeannie's lap to Sam's lap and stood on her hind legs looking intently through the window. Soon the Yorkie was barking loudly with ears alert while her little tail wagged furiously. Sam was elated at the apparent confirmation that he was not delusional.

But he was the only happy person in the cabin. The airplane was in an uproar. The baby screamed, the woman on the end yelled, the dog barked and the rest of the passengers began to complain loudly. The prude was wringing the bell for the attendant but there was no need. A flight attendant was making a rapid approach. For one mad moment, Jeannie wished the TSA agents had caught them in Philly. There was no telling what the price would be for in-air disturbance of a flight.

"What seems to be the matter?" The attendant asked calmly. It was the kind eyed woman who had offered them extra snacks.
"That idiot is making a commotion." The shriveled faced woman reported, triumphant in her joy of being able to report Sam. Sam was un-swayed by her derision.
"There are some people out there!" He insisted pointing out his window toward the wing of the airplane. "She sees them too!" he added indicating the alert Yorkie who had not looked away from the window. She had stopped barking but her tail seemed to be moving at the speed of the propeller. The flight attendant bent forward slightly and looked out the window.
"Those aren't people. Those are angels." she said matter-of-factly. "They are escorting us into London. I suggest you get some sleep. You are in good hands." She straightened up and walked off leaving the shriveled faced woman agape with a mixture of shock and dismay.

Jeannie looked curiously at Sam, unsure what to say. But somehow Sam seemed to settle down after that. The fear that had ridden the roller coaster in the pit of his stomach had been derailed. He napped peacefully, then watched the sky move from black to the deep orange hues of sunrise. The Yorkie on his lap never tired of looking alertly out the window. Together they marked the hours looking upon the mysteries of the skies.

Finally the moment of great anticipation arrived, when the captain announced the descent and the cabin crew busied themselves making sure seat belts were fastened, tray tables were stored and seat backs were upright. After all the magnificence of navigating thousands of miles suspended above the earth, the pilots were judged by the intensity of that final bump when the airplane's wheels first hit the tarmac. The pressurized cabin lost its magic and became a lesson in patience as hundreds of people waited to disembark.

LONDON

"Are you kidding me?" Sam looked in disbelief at the little four door SUV that was supposed to transport them and their luggage to Aunt Jen's apartment in Marble Arch. But in the end they stuffed Jeannie in the back seat surrounded by bags and Sam was left to face oncoming traffic driving on the wrong side of the road. Uncle Ned had greeted them warmly, if somewhat shyly as they exited Baggage Claim at Heathrow. He had seemed to be a meek and mild mannered man until he got behind the wheel of the car. Sam grasped the grab handle and squeezed his legs together, in an instinctive attempt to preserve himself and his progeny. The many roundabouts in lieu of traffic signals left Sam's hand cramped from the tightness with which he gripped the handle as he righted himself. There were obviously no hard and fast rules to driving in London and watching cars hurtling down the road at him on the left side of the road was disconcerting to say the least.

Uncle Ned zipped around the convoluted streets with an alacrity which was in strict contrast to his conversational skills. Sam was too stressed to talk. Jeannie pried Uncle Ned for information on Aunt Jen while keeping the carry-on luggage from slapping her in the head.

Aunt Jen was 47 and pregnant. She was Jeannie's youngest aunt. A rail thin and quiet woman of regal bearing, for whom life's usual milestones had been significantly delayed, Aunt Jen now found herself without the usual support systems typically afforded expectant mothers. She had spent much of her youth with her homely face buried in books and journals of an academic nature, making her an unlikely candidate for marriage. When Uncle Ned had finally come along with his horn rimmed bifocals, high-waisted pants and specificity in arachnid research, the couple did not waste time on a lengthy courtship. Each had instinctively understood that the Universe had finally given them a chance at happiness. They married quickly and without the frills typical of the virgin bride. The event had been eulogized by Jeannie's mother Sarah. She had insisted on flying over for her baby sister's nuptials despite her failing health and limited resources. Sarah had rounded up the family members and organized a delightful reception in the rose garden of the family church. Jen had been every bit the blushing bride. Ned had managed to fit the part of the dapper groom when Sarah had "accidently" dropped and stepped on his offensive glasses while pretending to compare them to the latest fashion eyewear in the local SpeedyService Optical Center. Ned had stumbled around like a blind moth until Sarah triumphantly led him into the technician's chair. She had spent a tidy sum on his new Christian Dior framed progressive transition lenses. The transformation had moved her as she had watched Ned look at himself in the mirror as if for the first time. He had touched his face with amazement at the attractive man he saw looking back at him.

That was five years ago. The recent news of Jen's pregnancy had struck a chord of panic in the family. Jen had kept it a secret for almost nine months for that very reason. At 47, the odds were high something would go wrong. But Sarah couldn't be there this time. Her own health concerns had grown significantly. When Jeannie volunteered to go in her place Sarah had been visibly relieved. Despite the distance, the bond between Jen and Jeannie had always

been strong. Deciding to surprise her Aunt, Jeannie had paid for
both Sam's and her own ticket without thought of her own needs.
So here she was in London for the first time since the wedding.
The baby was due any day now and Jeannie was ill prepared to
assist her aunt. She questioned her uncle cautiously.

"How is Aunt Jen doing?"

"Jolly good, I'd say."

"Has she been feeling okay?"

"Splendidly!" Uncle Ned gunned the accelerator as he propelled
the little car into the oncoming traffic of yet another round-about.
Sam was holding the "Oh God!" handle with both hands and sweat
was glistening on his forehead. Jeannie couldn't see his face from
her position in the back. At any rate, she would not have noticed
his discomfort. Her thoughts were on her aunt and how to crack the
code of politeness that was keeping her from learning anything
substantial.

"When exactly is the baby due?" Surely this was the best arrow in
her quiver of questions.

"Tomorrow." The reply was given so matter-of-factly that
Jeannie's response sounded hysterical.

"What??! Tomorrow??!!"

"Yes. She's in hospital now. We checked her in at 5 a.m. this
morning for tomorrow's 7 a.m. C-Section. You will see her
tomorrow."

Now that her questions had produced results Jeannie didn't know
what to do with the information.

She managed a weak "Oh."

Fortunately Uncle Ned zipped the car over to the side of the road,
came to a sudden stop and announced, "We are home."

When Jeannie walked into the hospital room the next morning,
Aunt Jen was lying under white sheets hooked up the IV. Her face
transformed with joy at the sight of her favorite niece. "Hello
Love! You are a sight for sore eyes! What a wonderful surprise.
"Did you fly all this way by yourself?" Aunt Jen's questions
tumbled over each other as she reached out to hug Jeannie.

159

"No, I brought a friend, Sam. He can't wait to meet you, He's in the waiting room."

"You mean that nice young man you've always told me about?" Aunt Jen asked. Jeannie said yes and they launched into a quick catching up on family news before Jeannie turned her full attention to Aunt Jen's belly rising from the bed like a giant mound.

"How're you doing Aunt Jen? Is everything alright?"

Aunt Jen said nothing for a long moment. The noises of the room asserted themselves; the rhythmic sighing noise of the blood pressure machine, along with the beeping and the ticking of various instruments that Jeannie could not identify. Finally Aunt Jen took a big breath,

"I am ready to have this baby," she said but her lips quivered a bit as she smiled.

"That is a good thing," Uncle Ned stood at the door dressed in scrubs, gloves and goggles, "They are ready for you in the operating room."

The wait seemed interminable to Jeannie and Sam. Since they were not next of kin they were not offered any information. Finally Uncle Ned appeared. Jeannie anxiously searched his face for answers but he looked shell shocked which could mean he had witnessed the miracle of birth, or something had gone horribly wrong.

"Uncle Ned, is Aunt Jen ok? Is the baby okay?"

"Yes, I think so." Uncle Ned stumbled over his thoughts, "she's asking for you."

When Jeannie entered the room Aunt Jen was holding a small bundle with tears flowing down her cheeks. Jeannie moved cautiously toward the bed not sure what to say.

"It's a boy," Aunt Jen whispered through her tears. Without waiting for Jeannie's response she continued. "He has 10 fingers, 10 toes, he has all his parts and he's beautiful..." she sobbed. Jeannie had the disquieting feeling that these were not tears of joy.

"He's perfect Aunt Jen. Let me hold him."

"Well perfect is relative." Aunt Jen whispered through her tears.

She turned the baby so his face was exposed to Jeannie. As she saw him her heart did a summersault. He looked just like Sam. Through the fog of mental processing she heard Aunt Jen's voice. "He has Downs Syndrome." Then she wailed, "Oh Jeannie, what kind of life will he have? Did I make a mistake bringing him into the world?"

Jeannie's head cleared with lightening brightness. She reached over and gave her aunt and the baby an awkward hug.

"No auntie. You didn't make a mistake. You didn't make a mistake at all. Please let me introduce you to my friend."

Aunt Jen looked a bit confused but nodded.

Jeannie went out and beaconed to Sam. He walked shyly into the room. Aunt Jen's eyes flew open wide at the sight of him. She immediately looked back at the baby, then looked back and forth several times. Sam gave a shy smile unsure what was going on. Suddenly Aunt Jen's face cleared like the sun coming out on a cloudy day. She looked down at her son and said softly,

"I see now. You are perfect." When she looked up she was crying again but this time joy shone through her tears. She smiled at Sam, beaconed him closer and said,

"Oh thank you Sam. Thank you for coming."

Sam looked quizzically from Jeannie to Aunt Jen for a moment but when his eyes rested on the baby's face he understood Aunt Jen's gratitude. He smiled and asked,

"What's his name?"

Aunt Jen didn't hesitate, "If it's alright by you, I think I'll call him Sam."

Just Pieces of You

I'm not as different as I seem
I'm just pieces of you
Floating in a dream.

161

Waiting in the Wings

I was born in an era of gentleness
On a stage of innocence.
But the props have fallen
The curtains have been drawn
Naiveté has been undone by a villain called Reality
But this bully cannot survive the final scene
For I carry the sacred seed of Faith in a world he cannot see
Look over yonder!
Even now Hope prepares her warriors
For a day when all my dreams take center stage.

Lost and Found

I would give all the things I've lost
to have the time back I spent searching for them.
I would pay you to take them away
Just to have the memories of how I lost them in the first place.
Searching is a sad way to live a life.
Looking down, brows in a frown, missing what's all around
Rather than searching for what's lost
I want to look at what is and find joy in what I still have.

Stress

Run run rush rush go go!
Crash, smash, wait, wait, oh no!

Bring the Dawn

The Price of Speed

Anxiously reaching for everything in the now
Our minds in perpetual unrest, we reach for more
Rearranging the molecules of life into warp speed
We trade time for effort until we are bankrupt of both
Paying for self-gratifying quickness with our only valuable coin;
Life.
Giving away what we can never get back.

The Unity of Man

Come back to love, all you who have a heart
Be young again, and foolish
Believe in wishes and dreams, hopes and themes
Laugh and dance, count the clouds and chase the sun
Work for the redemption of Truth.
Wait for the old and reach for the weak
Give credence to the Unity of Man.

Pretty Sunday

Sunlight streaming through the trees
Lifting my face to the gentle breeze
Canopied trees touching like eaves
Lots of time to just be.

Wake Up Call

Spirit called me sweetly
In the dark of my soul's night:

Bring the Dawn

Wake up little Dreamer,
There is work to do in the world of Men
Unclutter your soul
Let Silence take hold and free you from life's tyranny.

Spirit called me sweetly
In the dark of my soul's night
and offered me a way, a hope, a light.

Hidden Pages

Unfurl the Secret Scrolls
The Apocrypha of my Heart.
Unearth the Hidden Treasures of Being.
Take me beyond Believing
Awaken me to Knowing.

Somewhere deep in my Heart
You have written the Secrets of Our Love.
Take me there;
Away from the war cries of my mind
And the faltering doubts of my body.

Take me to the Silence
Take me to the Knowing
Take me to Peace.
Take me to Perfect Love which drives out fear.

Move me beyond the sound of Your Promises
To the Place where I lay my head upon Your Chest
And hear the Eternal Heartbeat of God.
Let that beat be the rhythm of my own heart,
Your Touch, the reality in which I dwell.
Amen.

Maze

Choice is the coinage of the century
Faith or doubt, anger or patience, fear or love
Each choice moves us along the maze of life.

Wave

There's a wave of newness
The poet rises with power and poise
Summer's ultimate manifestation of joy.

Painful Joy

Robin flittering through the trees
Mixing life and death with painful joy
Dew signifies the Robin's gone.

Ecstatic Dance

I'm not weird. Really, I'm not.

Weird events and people just seem to find me.

I am visiting North Carolina on business when I see a flyer advertising an evening of Ecstatic Dance on the notice board of a local restaurant. It is mid-winter so I dress warmly with boots, coat and all, don some lipstick and perfume and prepare to be entertained.

My first hint that something is off is when a calm, smiling soul greets me as I walk in and encourages me to leave my shoes and any non-essentials in a small room near the door. I am still determined to believe this is a typical dance recital.

They have wood floors for the dancers, they just don't want them ruined by high heels, I tell myself.

My next hint that something is amiss is a visual one. The chairs are all stacked on the side and the room is filling up with an assortment of people who seem content to sit in yogic postures or stand and sway like misplaced palm trees. They range from the budding flexibility and beauty of youth to the rigid stiffness of the aging. One man is wearing harem pants with horizontal multicolored pinstripes that sag around his thin frame like old drapery as he moves to a sound only he can hear.

Another, old enough to be my grandfather, is sitting erect with legs folded in a full lotus pose. What I don't see is any sign of a dance troupe or performers of any kind.

The calm smiling soul who greeted me at the door joins the group and we all sit in a circle on the floor. She tells us about reclaiming our grounding and connectedness to the earth through movement. She tell us to let go of our minds and be led by our bodies. Don't be self-conscious, she says. The group nods its assent. This is when I finally surrender my notions of being entertained. How is it they all know what's going on?

Bring the Dawn

In my mind I see the flyer tacked on the notice board. I am searching it for wording that would have told me I would be the subject rather than the watcher of the dance. But the flyer is dim in my mind, clouded out by assumptions. I am dressed to watch, not to dance and I have never seen these people before in my life. Who gets up and performs random dances in the company of complete strangers? But I am in the back of the room. The calm, smiling soul is looking at me with kind smiling eyes.
I'll wait until the music starts and sneak out with the other normal people who made the same mistake I made of expecting a dance performance. The thought comforts me, so I wait.

Apparently, I am the only normal person in the room because before the music starts everyone else gets up and claims a space to express themselves through the dance. There are men who appear to have survived Woodstock, their thinning graying ponytails speaking of freedom. There are women of every size and color claiming a space among the collective.
The music starts and one woman begins to prance with mincing steps. Her movements are reminiscent of the praying mantis. Another stands in place twitching and jerking like a malfunctioning robot. Another stares glassy eyed with a wide mouthed grin on her face like a lunatic. She is unmoving except for an occasional turn like a sunflower following the arc of the sun. I think to myself, God, I am with a bunch of weirdos.

I am not weird. Really, I'm not. But the music is like a heartbeat. It spurs action. My body wants to speak. It is drowning out the objections of my mind. So, I obey my body.
I'll slip out at the end of this piece, I tell myself.
I sway to the beat allowing my bare feet the luxury of intimate communion with the smooth cool oak floor. I still feel quite normal compared to the rest of the group. A plump young woman, in shorts that could well have been underwear based on their length, does pirouettes, twirling on her tip toe around the room. Sweat is already beading on the face of a heavy set man as he sets his arms

in motion as if conducting an opera. One of the Woodstock
refugees prances his way toward me opening his arms and his face
in a wide smile.
Yep. I'm the normal one even if I'm still here, I think.

The beat picks up the pace with urgency. It is calling for action.
But there is discordant movement all around me. I am black. I
pride myself on having the sense of rhythm inherent in my people.
This group is a mixture of madness and motion. But now it's my
heart that is overruling my head.
Those judgments are dead. Let go and flow.
I ignore the fact that my dress pants are snug. I move. And soon I
am swirling and twirling and bending like the other weirdos in the
room, having just as much fun.
But I can't be one of them, I tell myself. Look at her!
One woman flitters by me out of step with the music and
apparently with reality.
I have to draw the line somewhere. I'm not that weird.

My eyes find a slender beauty moving gracefully among the
disjointed mass.
There! That is the normalcy I seek. She is obviously a dancer.
But wait, is a dancer defined by level of performance or by intent
and action; by passion?
I am confusing myself with all this thinking. So I close my eyes
and go inside. I let my body move in joyful abandon, legs and arms
stretching and turning. Torso yielding, pulsating, flowing,
imitating the sounds like a mockingbird at sunset.

When the music stops I am the heavy set guy with beads of sweat
on my face. I am the Woodstock refugee with open arms and
smiling face. To top it off, the lunatic walks up to me and offers a
bottle of water and a towel. I take it them willingly with a smile.
I hope I am as weird as the ones I have judged.
I shake my head at my own hubris and smile.

Dance

Dance to catch pieces of yourself
That only appear
When you dance.

Cute Shoes

Hobbling across the parking lot
Late night ending in fierce throbbing pain
The price of cute shoes.

Tornado

An angry wind went down our streets tearing limb from limb,
It groaned and cried from house to house felling mighty trees.
It did not wait, it could not stand the sun's slow retreat from sight
So it tore down our transformers and ushered in the night.

Seasons

Summer draws to a close
All that's left is the choking humidity
And the swift thunderstorms
that rush in like a deranged lunatic,
destroying picnics, umbrellas and hope.

I look with longing for what has not yet bloomed
But Spring is long gone
Its daffodils and lilies, an all but forgotten joy.

169

Autumn awaits me; falling leaves and sagging hopes
Until Winter lays dormant every dream
and calls the warmth a liar.
Endless toil before me
For hopes that may well have already died
Within Summer's breathless grasp.

Snowball

Falling softy from the void of winter's blue
I blanket the earth with the wonder of the sky
I hang, I lay, I cover,
I stick, I melt, I stay
Unique with weightless beauty
I yield to gravity's seduction
rolling down the ice cold hill gathering momentum
Nothing, no one will match my speed
No one will merge with me
I must gather pieces of the earth and explode,
Or find a place to rest.
Alone.

The Depths of the Sea

What do you see? The sea asked me.
You judge me by my waves cresting before your eyes
By my calm and my fury, my ebb and my flow.
But what about what's unseen, deep down below?

Aahh, you judge me by what you see
The fish you eat, the boats I carry
The sands you see, where you can tarry
But what about what's deep down below?

Bring the Dawn

My oceans have rivers, my seas have streams
Deserts and canyons beyond your wildest dreams.
The water you seek resides in me,
Secrets unseen deep down below.

Longer than the rivers linking the seas
Deeper than the oceans floor, its mountains, its trees
There's a depth to me that starts at life's core
A wonder you have yet to explore.

Don't judge me by my waves cresting before your eyes
My calm, my fury, my ebb and flow
Come closer, don't be afraid, let's explore
There's so much to me, deep down below.

Live at the Confluence

Live at the confluence of Sound and Silence,
the place were all is one.
Stay at the source of contrast,
being aware of the branches of good and evil.
See the seed of beauty and of ugliness
before they sprout.
Detach from Drama
And be at Peace. - Tao 2

The Faint Call

Bits and pieces of a dream
Broken and floating in the stream
of a nightmare called life
Rushing and trying,
never being quite good enough to rest.
Always preparing for another test.
Time, the prison warden
Runs his night stick along your cell
Maybe this is no better than hell.

Or is the escape route an inside job,
The faint call, the distant yell
The whispers we don't hear so well
Of Freedom's salute to the soul's invincibility
In that place of incredulous possibility?

Uncle Don, Is it true that you are untouchable?

'The police did corner mi and beat mi right up yasuh.
What?! Did you file police brutality charges?
Well, mi did deserve it, yuh nuh see?
Why would anyone deserve to be beaten by the police?
Well, ina dem days I was a gangsta, yuh nuh see?
You?? A gansta, Uncle Don??!
Well I was a good gangsta, yuh nuh see?
What does that mean?
I didn't kill innocents, Man.
Did anyone try to kill you?
I-Man have never been shot. Jah protect I.'

<u>Jamaican Gangsta</u>

The Don knew this was the end. He closed his eyes, feeling the coldness of the revolver on the back of his neck. He briefly wondered if it was a .44 Magnum. It would be a shame to die at the hands of a less worthy weapon. He heard the click and waited calmly for the afterlife. Heaven or Hell, he had no regrets. He was a firm believer in karma. He had lived by the sword, now it was his turn to die.

But why was it taking so long?
He heard a second click; then a third. It slowly dawned on him that the weapon was not firing. It was stuck. That's what you get for using a cheap handgun, he thought with a hint of disgust. He heard his would-be assassin swear. The cold steel left his neck as the flustered gun man concentrated on his defective weapon. He pointed the weapon into the air and pulled the trigger again. This time the weapon discharged easily. But it was too late. A look of surprise registered on his face as Don's bullet entered his brain. Rule One: Always carry a back-up piece.

There were lots of rules in the Jamaican marijuana drug trade in the early 1980s. Rule Two: Don't over indulge in your own merchandize. That rule alone had cost many a dealer his business and his future; but not the Don. He built an empire on discipline. His yacht, cars, homes, jewelry and designer clothes were flashy indications of his wealth. But in truth he could have achieved much on looks alone. His unusually tall frame sported honey brown skin and handsome features framed with dreadlocks flowing neatly down his back. The striking combination guaranteed the Don an opening with many a woman. His steel grey eyes and fearless directness made him a force to be reckoned with many a man.

His cold ruthlessness in business was offset by the depth of his passion for life. His love for Stoli on the rocks and the crap tables was only surpassed by his love for women. He gave a helping hand to any who came asking, and they came in droves. As his wealth and reputation grew, scores wanted to be with him. Many wanted to be like him and a few wanted to be him. He welcomed them all into his circle, into his house and into the business if they so desired. Don had a tender heart for his impoverished countrymen. He never forgot his days of want. As a result his kindness endeared him to many, breeding a fierce loyalty that made him untouchable. Those who wanted to take his place one by one learned Rule Three: The morning sun should never find a traitor... alive.

Nobody could remember Don's real name. He had earned the title The Don after a shootout with rival drug runners in the hills of St. Andrew. Despite being surrounded by the Miami boys and their prolific use of semi-automatic weapons Don had come out blazing with his .44 Magnum. When the dust had cleared he was the only one unharmed. The members of his "posse" who made it out alive embellished the story with each retelling. His reputation took on a supernatural glow. He was "The Don". With the passing of time he simply became "Don".

After a while Jamaica was no longer big enough to contain his ambitions so Don migrated to the U.S. to control a larger portion of the drug trade. He explored Chicago, New York and DC, embracing the excitement of conquering new turf, and new women. In the wake of his American exploration he left a trail of broken hearts and white powder. He found that cocaine was not quite as forgiving as the ganja plant. When he woke up one morning, face down in his own vomit, bereft of his designer clothes, jewelry and the $500,000 he had collected from the last deal, he decided it was time to return to the basics. He had broken Rule Two. Now it was time to practice rule Four: Show no weakness. By sheer strength of will he distanced himself from the white demon but he had lost much of his credibility. He settled in Miami so that he could more easily control his shipments from home and rebuild his empire.

So in the end, it was not a bullet, an overdose or a prison sentence that took Don out of Miami. It was the fury of betrayed women. Women had loved him with passion and he had returned their adoration with gusto, too much gusto. His multiple liaisons had finally caught up with him. His wife, his girlfriend and his baby-mama all found out about each other. Somehow, despite the scores of women he had bedded, this three horned dilemma was his undoing.

He ran to Jamaica under the cover of night, avoiding the coast guards by a route through the Bahamas. He arrived on his yacht, with his Armani suits, his beloved Fedoras, a bank roll and what was left of his pride. He quickly built a small two story house overlooking the ocean on one of the many lots of land he owned. The news of the Don's return to Jamaica spread like wildfire. It had been over two decades but many still remembered the ruthless entrepreneur who stopped at nothing to get his marijuana shipments to his American distributors. If anything, time had added a legendary hue to his exploits. So night after night he was visited by every wanna-be and has been that searched the underworld for a foothold. Mixed into the heap were a few serious businessmen. They wanted what he had; connections to the Miami drug trafficking world. So for a time Don made his money referring growers to his overseas contacts. Still, his lust for the illicit was not assuaged by this hands-off approach.

He turned to cock fighting. Weekend nights found him in underground dives in the hills yelling obscenities at a game rooster who would fight to the death in mindless rage, not unlike that of its owner. And rage is what Don held in his heart. His multiple ex-wives and lovers had succeeded in closing the door of re-entry into the United States. They had enough details of drug deals, prostitution and gang involvement to put him away for the rest of his life, should he set foot on American soil again. He had no easily foreseeable future.

So Don sat in the sweltering heat of his un-air conditioned bungalow without a fan, pacing like a caged bull on sleepless nights. When he flew into rages, not unlike his fighting cocks, his neighbors wondered who else was in the house with him. But he spent his time alone except for the faithful hauntings of the neighborhood half-wit. He had been kind to Ronnie and for this he had earned his undying loyalty. Ronnie's self- appointed job was to pick up the pieces of his broken life and offer them back to him with quiet perseverance. Don broke his furniture, throwing fans, souvenirs, lamps and even his beautiful mahogany chairs over the two story balcony. When they landed, crashing below on the rocks of the all-knowing sea he found that his heart had not been freed from the confines of his actions. And so slowly, his paradise became his jail, reminding him daily of the transgressions that still bound him. Seven years penance on the island of his birth had turned into an anchor around his neck. He relived each decision, each drug deal gone wrong, each unhappy end to a love affair.

In this prison paradise he had gradually diffused some of his rage with the help of the blue green Caribbean Sea and the holy herb. His morning swim became a daily meditation. His marijuana smokes went up from a few joints each week to two or three joints per day. And though he was never really freed from his past he contemplated it from a detached corner of his mind with each inhalation.

It was during one of these meditative sessions that his cell phone rang with an overseas number. Before he knew it, Mona stood in from of him like a spirit conjured up from the smoke of the ganja plant. She was considerably older than he remembered. Although that was 30 years ago, it still unnerved him to see the years reflected on her face. It dawned on him that he must have aged too, but he was not prepared to face that reality...so he buried his misgivings in the softness of her still voluptuous body.

And so it was that he found again a ray of light in his darkened world, a spark of hope that somewhere beyond the ocean's edge he would once again enter into society, redeemed and refreshed.

Mona was a woman of action. She set to work to re-invigorate her defeated lover. Before he knew what was happening his prison paradise was up for sale, his fighting cocks were traded for a tidy profit and he was headed for the altar. Mona had been one of his first loves during his time of innocence before ganja and power had consumed him. He embraced her presence as a divinely ordained catechism in his quest for restoration. He marveled at the rapid changes in his life as he pulled out his collection of overstuffed Gucci suitcases. He pulled on a Christian Dior shirt and struggled to button it wondering how he would fit into his linen slacks in three days. He didn't want to walk down the aisle looking like the fat old man he had become. Looking in the mirror he rejected the image for the svelte slender frame he had taken for granted all his life. Maybe he could get back in shape, even start playing some soccer again. This woman is definitely good for me, he thought as hope again raised its timid head.

While Don rummaged through suitcases, a 747 touched down at

the distant Montego Bay airport. As he struggled with moth eaten clothes in his suitcases, the lone traveler easily collected his small black bag and slipped through security unnoticed. Despite the long scar on the side of his head he blended into the hustle and bustle of the airport crowd. He jumped into the waiting Escalade without a word. Two hours' drive into the hills of Negril and still no word was spoken. It was not from lack of trying on the part of the driver. Tony was being paid well to pick up the American and deliver him to the secluded house. But he was curious. Why the secrecy? He chattered the entire drive, hoping to get a hint of the stranger's purpose but his passenger sat in stony silence. The only communication from the traveler was the impatient drumming of his fingers on the passenger side armrest. The steady tapping for two hours almost drove Tony mad. When the car stopped outside the gate of the appointed address the traveler exited without even a nod. By now Tony was downright offended by the blatant rudeness. This offense along with his inquisitive nature demanded an answer. He pulled away from the curb, drove a few yards away then pulled his dark green Escalade into the bushes and waited to see what would unfold.

A staccato tap, a short wait and the gate swung open. The traveler disappeared inside the two story house surrounded by the lushness of mango, avocado and ackee trees. Tony did not see him hand over a roll of greenbacks in exchange for the short barreled Bushmaster semi-automatic. But he watched the automatic gate open slowly for a second time as a black BMW with tinted windows purred its way on to the road. At the wheel was the ill-mannered traveler. What is he up to? Tony had no idea but he knew who could tell him. He headed to his cousin's house, two miles inland. He worked for the owners of the two story house and had suggested Tony for the job of picking up the traveler.

The tale his cousin told took his breath away. Tony knew the Don well. They had played soccer together as boys. He had been in Don's wedding party when he married his first wife. He had driven

contraband many nights to Don's waiting propeller planes at the
end of dirt airstrips all over the island. He hadn't seen Don since
his fall into relative obscurity but he had heard all about the reason.
He made it his business to know what went on in the Jamaican
marijuana trade.

Meanwhile the traveler headed up the coast at break-neck speed.
He dialed an overseas number on his sleek black iPhone and
waited impatiently for the three women to all connect on the
conference call.

"I'm here," was all he said.
He drummed his fingers on the steering wheel while he waited for
the women to stop talking over each other. Finally one voice
emerged above the din.
"I want you to finish him off this time!"
Another voice piped in, "Don't leave that woman standing!"
The third voice was more tentative, "Well you don't have to kill
them..." The voice trailed off in the wave of backlash as the other
two shouted in opposition.
"We already agreed! That bastard did us all wrong! Now he wants
to marry another woman. No way!"
"Plus we already paid half the money for the job."
The traveler, tiring of the chatter, took his hand off the wheel for a
second to rub the scar on the side of his head.
"Stop the worrying. We have an agreement. This time I won't fail."
"Well it's not a good idea to talk about this over the phone," one of
the women was saying. He had already tuned them out.

He hung up the phone and continued to rub the scar with his free
hand. His jaw was set in a tight grimace. His eyes stared ahead but
he was seeing a night seven years earlier when his gun had failed
to fire. Those bickering biddies had come to him then as they had a
few days ago. They had wanted revenge then too. He had had no
beef with the Don. He had wanted only money then and if taking
out a womanizer brought in good dough that was fine by him.

When he ended up in the hospital intensive care unit for 91 days
they had been spooked. Rehab had been a long hard road. It took
him three years to regain full use of his left side. Some things still
didn't work right... One thing kept him going; the thought of sweet,
cold revenge. So when the same three women approached him for
a second time he didn't think twice. They had offered him even
more money than the first time. He took their money but he would
have done this job without payment. He had waited a long time for
this. Had he been a deep thinker he might have thought it ironic or
sensed a larger hand at work. But he was a cold, impatient,
humorless man with base and basic needs. It did not occur to him
that he had played a part in getting shot in the head. Guilt or
fairness were not a part of his make-up. But revenge, that was
something he could understand. It drove him to the point of
recklessness as he sped down the winding road toward his goal.

The day of the wedding dawned with an auspicious silence. Don
had sold his fighting fowls so the call-response of the roosters had
been replaced by the gentle lap of the sea as it kissed the shore
below the cliff. Ronnie bustled about the house and yard with laser
sharp attention to every detail. Don had chosen him to be his best
man and it puffed him up with his sense of importance. Don had
always looked out for him and treated him with the respect due an
equal. In return he had earned Ronnie's undying loyalty. He
watched over Don's roosters and his home without being asked.
And whenever there was news on the street he would faithfully
bring it to Don without the prejudice of his own interpretations.
Ronnie had a severe stutter which caused the village to brand him
as an imbecile. But Don was patient with the downtrodden and
disenfranchised. He had long since figured out the formula of
Ronnie's speech and could extract the essence long before the
casual observer understood a word.

Today Ronnie stuttered on about guests, food and liquor. He was
worried that since Mr. Bigga and Ms. Tiny (the neighborhood
moochers) would be at the wedding there would not be enough

food or alcohol. Don paid no attention to his concerns. He was surprised to find that despite having walked down the aisle several times he had a deep sense of unease. He put it down to pre-wedding jitters. It left him with no patience for Ronnie's jabber. He sent him off on a frivolous errand to give his nerves a rest.

"Go buy a few more bottles of White Rum at Ms. Murdy's shop, Man." Don stuffed several hundred Jamaican dollars in Ronnie's hand and almost pushed him out the gate. He knew the local shop keeper would be busy on a Saturday afternoon. The drinking had started the night before. By now it would be picking up steam. Ronnie was generally ignored by all except the children who occasionally taunted him. It would be a while before he got the attention of the shop keeper and even longer before he would secure the bottles of rum. That would buy him some time to smoke a joint and gain a few moments of peace. Don sat overlooking his backyard and the sea beyond wondering what the future held. Mona with her mysterious ways had secured a travel visa for him. His head held hope but his gut churned. After the second spliff of marijuana, he was in that mellow place that hid his fears. He heard Mona and her friends downstairs chattering and laughing. From the oohs and aahs he surmised she must have donned her wedding dress. He got up and headed to his room to get dressed. He looked at the linen suit on the bed and sighed at the struggle ahead of him. He was barely able to zip up the pants. He would have to watch his intake of curried goat once the vows were exchanged. He reached for his socks and grabbed the ankle holster for his back up piece by mistake. Old habits die hard, he thought to himself. He slipped on his Falke socks and walked out of the bedroom leaving the gun on the bed. Below the sound of chatter was growing louder. He quickly finished dressing and headed downstairs.

The Don's backyard overlooked the blue green Caribbean Sea. The sea glistened as tiny waves broke in the distance and the soft white clouds hovered above the horizon. White tents were interspersed along the edge of the cliff, bringing the horizon into focus like a 3-D projection. It was the perfect spot for a sea cliff wedding.

Mona was a woman of exquisite taste and Don's backyard reflected this. She had spared no expense in decorating the site of her wedding. Yet the display was a simple elegance, mirroring the beauty of the nature that surrounded it. The tents, tables and chairs were a blazing vision of white. There were blue green vases on each table with green ferns and hibiscus flowers of every hue. The wedding bouquet was a mixture of lilies and orchids draped with variegated bougainvillea. Long stemmed champagne glasses stood like sentinels at each place setting guarding the white china dishes rimmed with blue-green circles. White chairs seemed to spring out of the earth in rows decorated with blue-green bougainvillea. In front of the guest seating was a white wedding arch sprouting blue green petals amidst leafy green vines. To the left a four piece band played a soft mixture of instrumental reggae and calypso. To the right a row of tables stood covered with sparkling white table cloths. Large stainless steel containers sat on the white cloths. The bounty of the Caribbean peeked out from under the lids but the delicious aromas could not be contained. Curried chicken, escovitch fish, roasted breadfruit, fried plantains, ackee and codfish, rice and peas and jerk pork formed an aroma that would seduce the guests as the couple took their vows.

Don walked down to the edge of the cliff and stood in front of the minister, sweating slightly despite the cool sea breeze at his back. The ganja was wearing off. The unease in his belly was back. The guests were all seated, the minister waited, fully robed and exuding self-importance. Where the heck is Ronnie? Mona would be walking down from the house any minute now and Ronnie had not returned from his errand. As if summoned by his thought Mona stepped into view. She was like a mirage in the hot desert of his fears. She wore a simple white sleeveless dress which fitted her curvaceous figure then flowed from her hips in gentle swaying motions as she walked. Transformed by her joy, she exuded ageless beauty as she floated toward him. Don took her hand, mesmerized by her beauty.

"Raatid! "What wrong with dat damn fool?!"
The words cut through Don's hypnosis. He lifted his eyes from his
blushing bride to see his best man running down the hill toward
them at full speed. He was yelling a string of garbled words at the
top of his lungs. The wedding guests hissed at the disturbance but
Don knew better. His gut tightened and all his senses came into
sharp focus. Ronnie was stammering as he ran, a bottle of White
Rum in one hand and a black object in the other. Don saw the
object and grabbed Mona, throwing her to the ground behind him.
Mona screamed more at the sound of her ripping dress than at the
act of being dumped unceremoniously into the grass. Don held
both hands up high and Ronnie, reading the signal, threw the black
object. At that very moment the traveler rounded the corner of the
house, Bushmaster in hand and opened fire. The guests scattered
like leaves before a sudden wind, running this way and that. A few
like the minister jumped off the cliff into the sea below. The
traveler, in his hate and bravado, took the time to spray the tents
with bullets, shattering vases and china. But Don was focused, he
caught the .44 Magnum and fired.

Ronnie may have been slow of speech but his reflexes suffered no
defect. When the shooting started he ran into one of the tents
holding the bottle of White Rum above his head like a shield.
When a bullet shattered the bottle, dousing him with alcohol, he
dove under one of the tables inadvertently pulling it down over
him thereby creating a shield from the spray of bullets.

Don dropped to the ground and rolled away from the chairs filled
with his wedding guests. Instead of hiding under the protection of
the people he moved toward the food to pull the gun fire away
from the people. The traveler showed no such regard and would
have mowed down everyone in sight if one of Don's bullets hadn't
ripped through his sleeve. He could shoot the crowd later, he
reasoned. He turned his attention to his original target. Bullets

pinged off the shiny chafing dishes steaming with hot joyful foods.

Ms. Tiny, whose nickname belied her size, was matched in girth and appetite by her aptly nicknamed husband, Mr. Bigga. Sitting in the front row gave them a moment to think out their exit strategy when the shooting started. They looked over at the steaming buffet of curried goat and rice and peas and looked back at the gun man. Then they looked at each other. Thirty years of marriage and shared meals left them in full harmony when it came to food. In a split second they wordlessly acted on one accord rushing the traveler from opposite sides. The gun man was so busy focusing on Don he didn't see the tag team until it was too late. His brain had trouble processing the fact that an unarmed fat woman would be running at him while he was holding and firing a semi-automatic weapon. Had he the depth he would have thought of his own mother. Instead he paused long enough to reject any pull of filial ties. It registered that this woman seriously intended to run into him. He snarled in contempt and turned his weapon on her. Before he could take aim his world shook with the force of an earthquake, the gun went flying and he was lying on the ground. "What the...?" He would have picked himself up off the ground but the 400 pounds that had knocked him over reached down and put the full force of his weight into a punch to his face. He vaguely saw rather than felt a huge and terrible weight descending on him as he blacked out. When the mayhem subsided Mr. Bigga was holding the weapon and Ms. Tiny was sitting on the hapless traveler.

Don, seeing that the gun man had no chance of escape, ran to Mona. Her dress was ripped and grass stained and her freshly coiffed hair was somewhat askew but she was none the worse for wear. He helped her to her feet and held her close. The moment of intimacy was interrupted by thunderous applause. The guests who remained on the property, behind the house, various trees and the chicken coop, had all re-emerged and were expressing their approval of Ms. Tiny and Mr. Bigga's bravery. Ronnie popped up from the floor of one of the tents and seeing the coast clear, ran over to Don. All eyes turned to Ronnie as he told Don what precipitated the events. For the first time in his life Ronnie found he had an attentive and patient audience.

It turned out that Tony, having learned the purpose of the traveler's plans from his cousin had taken it upon himself to locate his old friend before the traveler did. He no longer had a telephone number or exact address. He had made his way across the island to where his sources told him the Don was currently living. He was in Ms. Murdy's shop asking for Don's exact location when Ronnie walked in and overhead him. As he paid for the White Rum Ronnie had listened carefully to Tony asking about a black BMW with tinted windows. He had walked by the very same car on his way to the shop. It had prowled by him as if in search of something, or someone. When it dawned on Ronnie that Tony was in danger he had slipped out of the shop and ran into the house to warn him. Tony was below waiting but his revolver was lying on the bed. Ronnie had grabbed it and raced downstairs, just as the black BMW pulled up to Don's gate. When the story unfolded to the current moment there was another thunderous round of applause, this time for Ronnie. He suddenly looked confused and bashful. Never before had his community seen fit to praise him.

Once Don got the full story he was livid. He whipped out his cell phone and made an overseas call to a number he had not dialed in years. His unsuspecting ex-wife, seeing a Jamaican area code on her phone, got ahead of herself.
"Is he dead?" She said as she opened the conversation.
"No. He is very much alive!" The venom in Don's voice caused her blood to run cold. He didn't wait for her to recover. "Get the other two on the line." He waited for the conferencing effort to be complete then he spoke again. "This has gone on long enough. I made a mistake. Heck! I made many mistakes and I hurt each one of you, for this I am sorry. If I could take back the past I would but all I can give you is my apology. I lost the joy of watching my children grow up because of my mistakes. I am moving on with

my life. It's time for you all to move on as well. Seven years is long enough! I am sending your boy back to you alive, this time. But know that if you come after me again I won't be so kind. Revenge runs in two directions. If I even suspect that this is not over, you will each find yourselves facing charges. My boys in Miami are watching each one of you." He ended his soliloquy with a deliberately long silence. The women for their part, were stunned. Not only had they failed but now they might be in danger. The fact that Tony's gang had disbanded years ago and his only "boys" consisted of a village idiot turned hero and a few hungry wedding guests did not reveal itself to the women. They nervously agreed to his demands, even apologized.

He hung up the phone with a sense of having taken care of some long neglected loose ends. His relief was palpable. He had not realized the weight he had carried all these years until he apologized to these women. Wow; such a simple act carrying so much power.

Don walked back down toward the tents. The wedding guests had hung around, the thought of the curried goat and other delights had filled them with patience. By now the traveler had been tied up against the breadfruit tree at one corner of the property. The minister and several others had swam to the rocky cliff steps and made their way back to the scene. The minister took his place under the wedding arch, trying hard to look dignified in his wet robes.

Don looked at him and shook his head. "What happen to your faith when the shooting start, Man?"
"Well it's like Bob Marley say Man, 'He who fight and run away, live to fight another day'."
Don shook his head and reached for Mona's hand, "You still want to marry a reformed gangsta?"
Mona blushed with joy, and stepped up to his side,
"Yeah Man!"

186

The Art of Personal Warfare: A Series

The First Battle

To learn to fight
is to detach from violence
Rule One of fighting:
know when to retreat.
Not every battle should be fought
But if you must fight
decide from the stillness of who you are
not the noise of circumstance.
The victory in each battle
is not in defeating the enemy without,
It is in conquering the enemy within.
When you can see your own death,
Remain calm and not be alarmed,
Your enemy cannot defeat you
because you will have detached from violence
by conquering your own fear.

Violence

The fist in your face is but a tentacle of violence,
an end result of a destructive course.
Its root lies in a thought
Which must first defeat and destroy
All hope of peace, all acts of love, all reconciliation
This thought must grow in the mind,
Poisoning the pathways that lead to action.
And so every act of violence begins with self-hatred
It starts with the unholy 'I' being enthroned in the seat of 'Right'
And the dethroning, the destroying of another.

War's Reason

True Warfare's ultimate purpose is unification
Not destruction.
If we first conquer the thoughts and actions
that cause disharmony in our own lives,
Then we can take back the land
where who we are is in sync with what we do.

Sparring Match

***Stand**; rooted in the Unseen*
***Move!** like lightening before the thunder*
***Strike!**, in the power of certainty*
***Block!** with a resounding 'No!'*
***Yield!** with the balance of the wind*
***See!** what is, before it is born*
***Retreat!** like one never there*
***Rest**; leaving all effort to the Unseen.*

Homelessness

Wandering the endless night of pain
He breathes the shallow droughts of a drowning soul
He seeks a home for his soul
He longs to be made whole.

Caught in the gossamer of doubt
Each touch, each kiss, each liaison,
A search for a deeper belonging.
Finding instead a nameless longing;
Love's mirage of empty promises.

A strong and arrogant man without,
A broken heart and fears within.
He shouts, he fights, he leaves, he lies
He drinks, he shoots, he dies.
Inflicting pain to hide his own
For there is no home for his soul.

WBDJ-7 TV Roanoke Virginia Shootings

What will it take for them to listen?
What do we need for us hear?
What will make me pay attention?
When will we heed what's near?

People are dying in the streets
Being killed before our eyes
Beheaded, blown up, shot
But we wait for someone else to act.

Still they're rushing, won't take stock

Bring the Dawn

We do not pause to hear our hearts' cry
I do not grieve beyond the cursory shock.
It's business as usual after the latest attack.

9/11

To all who say
"Never Forget"
I say,
Never Forget Why.

The Seed of Terror

Terrorism doesn't just burst through a door
or show up on airplanes
it starts as a seed in each mind,
a thorn in each heart
It grows when hope dies
and the will to control becomes the ultimate goal.

God's Friend
(Duality)

Would it shock you if I said,
'The Devil is closer to God than you are?'
Would it offend you if I said,
'He and God are better friends?'
For you spend your life trying to get closer to God
While the Devil spends time in His Presence.
You hope to hear a Word from God
While they talk all the time.
And while the Devil does God's bidding
You resist the pain and hardships of your life.
But all the while the Devil and God are in agreement
Trying to teach you
That there is no Duality.
There is only One.
(Job 1:6-12; 2:1-6)

Bring the Dawn

There is a hope that comes from the joy of innocence;
This is not that kind
There is a hope that comes from wishing and blind desire;
This is not it.
This is the Hope that comes from pain and struggle.
It is the Hope born of a Darkness that tears cannot dispel.
This is the Hope that rises up in everyone
Who has ever challenged what is and demanded what must be.
It is the only Hope that can light the Darkness of our souls.
It is the Hope that Brings the Dawn.

===

Dixie Ann Black

Dixie Ann Black is a poet, author and public speaker.
Her passions are health and fitness, education and world travel.
She is an avid seeker of Truth and its application to daily life.
She was born and raised in the beautiful island of Jamaica. She
lives in Florida.
Dixie is also the author of ***Just Chasing the Sun***,
A Unique Collection of Short Stories and Poems.

She can be reached for readings and speaking engagements at:
DixieAnnBlack@gmail.com.

Made in the USA
Columbia, SC
19 January 2019